There is a Season

G.W. Allison

There is a Season

For Kerry. Always.

CHAPTER ONE

Tom Hatcher sat in the last row. He was alone and throughout the worship portion of the service, he didn't sing nor did he clap along. Tom barely wanted to stand. The band was loud. The lights were dim. The giant media screens with bursting clouds of lightning and lyrics helped the people follow along like a well-rehearsed choir. They raised their hands. Some wept and others looked to heaven, or the ceiling, depending on whether or not you were an observer or partaker in the melodic offering of the service. The congregation sang with exuberance that Tom wished he had just a small portion of, reassurance that he was capable of an emotion other than anger.

It was a contemporary church. It was a

church where blue jeans and sneakers outnumbered ties and slacks three to one. It was a casual church in appearance, but in devotion, they were zealots of the usual sort. It was a Pentecostal church, which meant they believed in the active pursuit and movement of the Holy Spirit, part of the big three of the Holy Trinity. As in the days of old recorded in the book of Acts, Pentecostals depended on the power of that spirit to help them as agents of God on Earth. According to the Bible, the Holy Spirit empowered them with signs and wonders, and counseled them in times of need. He gave believers words to speak and wisdom to live.

However, as the service went on, there were no tongues of fire resting on the heads of the people, as it was on the day of Pentecost some two thousand years ago, though they did pray fervently. A mighty rushing wind did not sweep down from the heavens, bestowing power from on high, though they eagerly anticipated and expected such an occurrence. What they did have was an air of humility and the overwhelming desire to stand in the

4

presence of God. It was in the way they sang their songs, how they reached to heaven as if almost touching the fingertips of the Almighty reaching back to them. They sang as if God stood among them, tapping his foot to the beat and moving through the crowd, whispering in their ears the answers to their late night prayers. If there was one thing that the Pentecostals did not lack, it was faith and it was the reason Tom had decided to go there on this early Sunday morning.

During the greeting time, which someone from the stage called a time of connection, Tom remained planted firmly in his row. He stood rigid and only shaking the hands of those next to him. He was in no mood to hobnob. Two or three fake smiles and firm handshakes was all he was willing to handle then he took his seat and he waited. He waited for God to speak to him. It did not happen during the song service, even though he thought God would have chosen such a dramatic moment. Rarely do people actually get a soundtrack during one of their most desperate hours and God loved to make a theatrical point, or so Tom thought. The Bible was a badly written melodrama, as pretentious as an English play. But it did not happen during the song service, not even a hint, despite the emotions of those around him. So, he waited. Tom was all ears and he still anticipated a miracle. It was all he had left and he was willing to sit through anything to get one.

The pastor of the church took center stage. His name was Dan Underwood and he wore ironed blue jeans, a sweater vest, and penny loafers. Dan smiled, his teeth too big for his mouth, and asked everyone to sit.

"It's good to be in the house of the Lord," Dan said.

The people responded with amen and Pastor Dan produced an envelope. He held it up for all to see.

"This past Friday, the church was updating its health plan for the staff," he said. "And for most of you it is a time of worry, not knowing whether the company is going to cut some benefits or 'tweak' the plan. As I was sitting there deciding what was best in these hard economic times, I asked God for his help, like many of you do. If you're like me, you start thinking about all the things that could go wrong with the kids, your wife, or yourself as you get up in age. You start worrying about where you're going to get the extra money for health costs. And the Lord reminded me by saying, 'Take a look at your kids.' And I looked out the window into my backyard and saw my two boys running around, playing and climbing trees, just being boys. And God said to me, 'Haven't you come so far? Have faith.'"

The people responded with amen and Tom rolled his eyes. He adjusted in his seat. He was anticipating a bad reaction to whatever Pastor Dan was about to say next.

"So, I say to you, have faith and continue in that faithfulness," he continued. Then he prayed, "Father, we are grateful and we look back on our lives and know that you are proven, that you are a faithful God, a miracle worker. We're going to talk about miracles today and, God, for some of us it's a real act of faith. And for some of us it doesn't make sense. It doesn't add up in our checkbooks and we need you to intervene. We come to you with faith today, believing that you are a miracle worker. And, God, I pray that you begin to spring up in our hearts more and more faith to do the things we talked about last week. Help us to go above and beyond our tithes and offerings, because it's not just about us. Work in our hearts and our prayers, Lord, so that we can work towards furthering your kingdom. Amen."

"Amen," the people responded.

Tom felt a flash of heat rush to his face. A pit formed in his stomach when Pastor Dan said that God was a miracle worker. Before he knew it, Tom stood and raised his arm, his hand high like a schoolboy wanting the teacher to call on him.

"Yes, friend?"

"Where?" Tom asked.

"Where what?" Dan said.

"Where are the miracles? When will he reach down from his ivory throne and touch the people?"

The room fell silent but for the hum of amplifiers from the stage. All eyes were on Tom. He saw the surprise in their eyes. Some of them had awkward smiles. They were probably anticipating a visual lesson of some sort, a dramatic display of a point to help the pastor introduce his message. But there were others that scowled, knowing full well that a somewhat familiar face, they couldn't quite put their fingers on it, from the back row had the audacity to question the one that blessed them with new cars and abundant square footage for them to throw insatiable holiday parties and celebrations in his name.

Tom saw a couple of thick-necked ushers approached him out of the corner of his eye, but he didn't care. One of them gently placed his hand on his elbow and Tom snapped a look at him then yanked his arm away. The ball was rolling and it was going downhill. There was no stopping it.

"I want to know! I want to know where God is! You sing songs! You give money, time, blood, sweat, and tears! You talk about faith and being faithful, but when it comes down to our absolute desperate needs, God is nowhere! So, when and where? When will the Almighty take time out of his busy schedule and actually address our needs?"

Tom felt rabid. He wanted to grab Pastor Dan and shake him. He wanted to stand on his chair and scream. He wanted someone to give him a sliver of hope. But mostly he wanted God to assure him that he was there. He did not want to be comforted for comfort's sake. He wanted to confront the one who held the whole world in his hands. He wanted to look into the eyes of a god who claimed compassion in stories written about men and women who thought the world was flat and stoned people to death when they stepped out of some holy line. The whole thing sounded insane to Tom, but he wanted to see for himself whether God would strike him down for his arrogance. He wanted to see if God would challenge his unbelief. It was a last resort. Life did not need to prove its reality. Its pain was evidence enough. Let the Almighty announce his presence with pain then. At least Tom would know that there was a god, that there was hope for the hopeless. But Tom knew that it wasn't going to happen. It never did. And the man on the stage would be the one to withstand the worst of it.

The congregation turned their eyes from Tom to Dan. He was standing there silently. He held his hands folded tight against his stomach. It was unfair of Tom to take advantage him like that out in the open and Tom knew he had questioned the pastor's pride as well as his beliefs. But he also knew that the pastor would not miss the opportunity to seize upon a possible Sunday morning miracle. He was sure of it. After all, why would God allow such an outburst, but to test the faithful and the faithless? It was a moment that these types of men romanticized, but rarely found themselves entangled. It was an opportunity to practice before an undivided audience what he had always been preaching. This was a defining moment for him as a leader and for the church and for Tom, the poor sap that was desperate for an answer. Dan stepped down from the stage and made his way up the center aisle to the back row where Tom stood.

Tom heard some people praying. He

heard them ask God to touch him, to reveal his glory to him, and some asked God to remove this man from their presence. Most, however, continued to watch as their pastor placed his hand upon the stranger's shoulder.

"Friend, I know there are questions and I know there are hurts."

"You have no idea," Tom said.

"It is by faith we are healed. We must have faith."

He heard it all before. The evangelists on the television, the chapel at the hospital, they all said the same thing. They were clanging cymbals, all of them. Their words were nothing but noise to break up the uncomfortable, silent anguish of a man gripping the edge of a crumbling cliff.

"Isn't the very act of prayer faith in itself?" Tom asked. "Talking out loud to an invisible being, hoping he'll hear you and somehow help you. I'm all out of faith."

Dan nodded and pulled his lips tight and

furrowed his brow as he tried to show Tom
he was deeply concerned for him, that he
understood the desperation in his voice.

"You have to believe that you believe with
all of your heart," Dan said. "There can be no
doubt, for doubt is the yeast that spoils the
whole loaf."

Tom flexed his jaw and sighed heavily. He
shook his head and fought back the words
he wanted to scream in the pastor's face. The
last thing he wanted to hear was some
Christianese spiritual babble that was
meaningful only to some head-in-the- clouds
Jesus freak. Tom pulled back from Dan. It
was too much for him. He wanted to burst
into the very throne room of heaven and
grab God by his white robe. He demanded
an answer and only received nonsense. So,
he settled for the next best thing and
slammed his fist into the preacher's nose,
sending him to the ground.

"You believe that?" Tom shouted.

The ushers grabbed Tom and pulled him
back. Women in the congregation screamed,

some wept loudly and moaned, "Jesus! Jesus! Jesus!" A man with muttonchops that would have made Elvis cringe helped Dan to his feet and asked if he was okay. Dan wiped away the blood and looked around at the faces staring   back at him. The lily-white suburbanites of the congregation had never witnessed such a thing. No doubt they thought the world, indeed, was full of animals and it was going to hell in a hand-basket.

"It's okay. I'm okay. God is in control."

The ushers held on to Tom tightly. He struggled as Dan wiped away the tears in his eyes and shook off the sting of the punch. It was more than a blow to his nose and to his ego. It could shake the very faith that some of the fence walkers held on to. He had to save face, Tom knew, and he had to capitalize on the moment, but how, Tom didn't know. Pastor Dan stared at Tom. He was indifferent then compassionate then angry.

"Call the police."
The ushers dragged Tom from the

sanctuary. In the foyer, a fellow that went by the name Big Mac threw Tom to the ground and sat on him while another usher called 9-1-1. Now, on top of everything else, Tom was going to jail and he had never felt so alone.

CHAPTER TWO

The jail cell was a cinder-block room with a solid steel bed frame and thin rubber mattress. In the corner was a stainless steel sink and toilet without a seat. There was a narrow window with thick glass recessed into the wall that looked out into the parking lot of the adjacent courthouse from the third floor. It was Tom's only assurance that the world continued to turn. Echoes of angry men screaming for their one phone call bounced off the walls. It was cold and the florescent lights stained the room a greenish hue. Tom sat on the steel bed and buried his head into his hands. He wanted to cry, but he couldn't.

Three years ago, he had been riding a wave of success. Tom and his family moved

to the Village of Clarkston, a tiny collection
of historic homes in North Oakland County,
Michigan. It was a stark contrast to Florida,
but a job at a local Detroit news station
where he anchored the weekend desk for
their morning show was a big step in his
career. The morning show was a small
production that tried to emulate the Today
Show and featured local celebrities and
happenings around town. The money was
twice that of his previous job in Hick Town,
Florida. And with their new found success,
Tom and his family bought a historic home
on Main Street, an adorable blue Victorian
house that his wife Sarah fell in love with
before they even stepped inside.

Sarah spent their first summer
redecorating the house while their daughter
Tiffany, then four, chased ducks in the
backyard along the Old Mill Pond. They
took walks down to Rudy's Market to get
ice-cold Faygo pops that you had to open
with a bottle opener. There was a parade on
Memorial Day and another one on the
Fourth of July. Tom and Sarah watched the
parades from their porch while Tiffany
scrambled for tossed candy from the floats of

local businesses, politicians and fire trucks. The firefighters sprayed the children going for the candy with water pistols and Tiffany cried because her candy was wet. The downtown park with the small creek running through that fed Old Mill Pond had a festival every weekend and they sat and listened to jazz and folk music while being entertained by a clown or two.

The fall brought Halloween. Ghosts and spider webs adorned the town as little ghouls and goblins ran from house to house begging for treats. Tiffany was a fairy and she tossed apples into the pond and devoured the chocolate before mom or dad could say no. Thanksgiving was as traditional as they come. Sarah's parents flew up from the Sunshine State. Mom helped Sarah cook while Dad sat by the fireplace watching the Detroit Lions get eaten alive by a hungrier team then sang silly songs as Tiffany hopped around like a little monkey saying, "Again, again, again!" Afterward, they all sat on the front porch drinking hot cider and they waved to neighbors walking their dogs before settling in for the night.

At Christmas time, the town was aglow with lights and plastic snowflakes hanging from the street lamps. Christmas carols filled the air from Rudy's outside speakers and, once again, Tom and Sarah watched another parade from their porch as Tiffany dodged snowballs thrown by neighborhood children. On Christmas Eve, Tom and Sarah sat by the fireplace after placing Tiffany's gifts under the tree and sipped wine while Bing Crosby sang the Hawaiian Christmas Song, their favorite. It was pure Americana and life could not have been sweeter.

Then things started to change in the second year. They settled into the community. Tom was a minor celebrity now. He spoke at special events, charities mostly, offering a bit of local television flash for audiences. It felt ridiculous, but he kept getting invitations.

Sarah started getting headaches. She had always been a picture of health, so as the headaches became more frequent, they both grew more concerned. The family doctor diagnosed her with migraines, that mysterious catch all for throbbing, vomit inducing head busters. She popped the prescribed pills like candy and Sarah often joked that taking them would be more fun if they were in a Pez dispenser. The pills didn't help, though, and the headaches grew worse.

On the day before they went to the emergency room, Sarah had a fever and her body ached. On top of the headaches, she thought she had the flu and stayed in bed the whole day. Tom called off from work to be with Tiffany. She felt bad and insisted that he go. The morning show's guest was Bob Segar, a musical hero of Tom's. He stayed home and he and Tiffany made Sarah chicken soup. She never touched it. When she finally fell asleep, they tiptoed around the house and spoke in whispers so they wouldn't wake her. The next day, the fever had risen to a hundred and three. Sarah had been vomiting all night and morning. By the afternoon, all that was coming up was bile and blood. They needed to go to the hospital.

Three hours and forty-two minutes after arriving at the emergency room, a young Indian doctor named Ashwin Mehta, not long out of medical school and probably the pride of her family, entered the waiting room.

"Mr. Hatcher?" Doctor Mehta asked.

Tom was asleep with Tiffany draped over him, drooling on his shoulder. He awoke and blinked away the fuzziness of the nap.

"Mr. Hatcher, I'm Doctor Mehta. Do you mind if we talk for a moment?"

Tom nodded and gently laid Tiffany on an empty couch. She stirred for a moment and he brushed back her hair and told her to go back to sleep. She whimpered then drifted back to dreamland where unicorns and monkeys were probably singing her songs. Tom and Doctor Mehta stepped out into the hallway.

"How is she?" Tom asked.

"She's better. Stable. We've given her an IV to replenish her fluids. The vomiting dehydrated her quite a bit. Also, she's been given some Tylenol for her headache and fever."

"She gets really bad migraines."

"Sarah was complaining of abdominal pain when you brought her in?"

"She was vomiting."

"I ordered blood and urine tests for her and we gave her a CT scan. The tests aren't back. Mr. Hatcher, there appears to be a growth on her right kidney."

Doctor Mehta let that sink in for a moment before she continued. Tom was trying to process the information. He nodded and looked into Doctor Mehta's eyes.

"We won't know much until the blood and urine tests are back. I've also ordered a biopsy of the growth."

"But her doctor said she had migraines."

She didn't respond and Tom knew what she was thinking. The doctor was wrong, but professional courtesy wouldn't allow her to say it. Plus, this was still a guess. So far, all they had was a CT scan. It could be nothing

or could be something. That was all they
knew. There was no point in badmouthing
the family doctor.

Doctor Mehta scribbled onto some
paperwork then looked up at Tom. She had
large round eyes that were deep and dark. It
was a good look for a doctor that dealt with
as much bad news as good news. She had a
good bedside manner.

"Don't worry too much, Mr. Hatcher.
Once we've determined what the growth is,
we'll talk about treatment, if any. Best-case
scenario, it's nothing. Worst case, it's cancer,
which means she could lose the kidney."

"But, we still don't know anything?"

"Yes, however…"

"You've seen this before?"

"I'm an oncologist, Mr. Hatcher.
Unfortunately, I see this more than I care to."

"What else?"

"We'll give her an MRI to see if there are any growths or abnormalities elsewhere. I'll let you know the results once I have them. Until then, we hope and do all that we can to help Sarah."

Tears welled up in Tom's eyes and he blinked them away. He looked back at Tiffany sleeping on the couch and the tears came back, this time slipping over his eyelashes and onto his cheeks. Doctor Mehta placed her hand on his arm and squeezed it.

"You can go in and see her. She's awake, but a bit groggy." "Thank you, Doctor."

But it was not a best-case scenario. And it was the worst of possible scenarios. In just two weeks, Sarah was dead. She had Renal Cell Carcinoma and it rapidly spread throughout her body without her or the family doctor knowing. What the doctor thought was just a headache was really the end for Sarah. Like a thief in the night, cancer crept in and stole her life before she even knew it was gone. Sarah's own independence and stubbornness took her life in the end. She didn't want to worry anyone when she first started noticing the pain in her back, which even then was part of the final assault. She chalked it up as the price of getting older, even though Sarah was only thirty-five.

When she noticed blood in her urine the first time, she told herself it was only the remnants of her menstrual cycle and that she need not worry. By the time the headaches began torturing her, it was too late. The day Sarah died, Tom and Tiffany could only watch as she slipped into a coma, struggled through her final breaths, then stop. At the ICU desk, nurses and physicians openly wept as the echoes of little Tiffany's cries for her mommy to come back filled the hallways. Never did Tom think he would ever experience a more heartbreaking moment in his life.

It was at least six months before some sort of normalcy returned to the Hatcher home. Tom hired a nanny to help take care of Tiffany after school. Kindergarten was bitter sweet for both of them. Sarah was looking forward to the first day of school as much as Tiffany. Tom cried as he hugged Tiffany on the steps of Clarkston Elementary. Tiffany, always a bit on the precocious side, told her dad that it was supposed to be a happy day and that they should think only happy thoughts. Tom smiled and agreed then sent her on her way. He then went home, crawled into bed, and tried to sleep the day away.

The same week that Tiffany started school, Tom stepped down from his anchoring position to take on the roll of an investigative reporter. The hours were more flexible, allowing him to be home when Tiffany needed him. It came with a slight decrease in pay, but it was a small silver lining in what Tom called the cloudy months. He was grateful and took assurance in knowing that he could do anything in the news business. The old life appeared to have returned as much as it could. He and Tiffany started to do the things they used to do. They went on picnics in the park, watched the parades, and Tiffany fed and chased ducks along the shore of Old Mill Pond.

During Thanksgiving, Sarah's mom and dad flew up to spend the weekend with their only grandchild. Mom overcooked the

turkey and burst into tears. Dad sat by the
fireplace and paid little attention to a new
and unstoppable Detroit Lions team. He only
sang one silly song for Tiffany, but she
didn't dance. Instead, she crawled up into
his lap and rested her head on his chest. His
heart was not in it and she could tell. There
was no hot cider on the porch as they spent
the evening looking at picture albums,
crying, laughing, and telling stories about
Sarah. Later, when the house was dark and
everyone was in bed, Tom heard Sarah's
mother and father crying in the guest room
down the hall.

On Christmas, a day Tom dreaded, things
somehow looked brighter. Rather than
spend the holiday in the house that Sarah
built, Tom and Tiffany surprised Grandma
and Grandpa by showing up on their front
porch with an arm full of presents. They
were the hit of the retirement community as
every blue haired old lady within a mile of
Tiffany pinched and kissed her cheeks and
every bald-headed old man wanted to have a
beer with Tom. There was little time for
sadness and it was good for everyone. At the
airport, Sarah's mom squeezed Tom and

thanked him for everything. There were no tears, only smiles, and life was finally moving on.

Then on the morning of New Years Day, the hill took a dramatic slope downward. Tiffany's screams from the bathroom startled Tom so that he fell from his bed, hitting his head and dazing him for a few moments. Her screams grew louder and she started to yell, "Daddy!" He hurried to his feet and burst into the bathroom to find Tiffany standing against the wall with tears streaming down her face.

"What? What, Tiff?"

Tiffany pointed to the toilet and Tom cautiously approached, not knowing what he was going to find. He felt his knees shaking. He gripped the sink to keep from buckling then Tiffany grabbed him around the waist, burying her head into his side. He realized that he was hyperventilating and he made a conscious effort to stop. Tom took one more look in the toilet bowl to see the blood and urine before calling the doctor.

He specifically requested Doctor Mehta. When she took him to a private room, his greatest fear gripped him by the soul. She told Tom that his only daughter of five years of age had Renal Cell Carcinoma, a rarity among children. Tom was lost. With no one to turn to and no one to comfort him in that moment, he collapsed onto Doctor Mehta's shoulder and sobbed until he thought he would die himself. Doctor Mehta held him, but said nothing. She didn't need to.

The next two weeks played hell on Tom. Doctors poked and prodded his little girl like a science experiment. He talked to so many doctors that it started to become comical. At one point, while being debriefed by a room full of white coats after one of Tiffany's CT scans, Tom did his best at suppressing a laugh, eventually failing. He fixated on the number of foreign accents coming at him all at once and lost control. The doctors were not amused and finally left him alone in the room, giggling like a crazy man.

There was a spot of good news during that time. They caught the cancer early enough and at the end of those two weeks, Tiffany had her right kidney removed. She spent another week in the hospital for recovery then continued for a few months at home in outpatient care. The time at home proved to be just as difficult, if not more, though. Tiffany often cried at night, keeping Tom awake, and making the days long and stressful. The nanny came in the afternoons to give him a much-needed break that he rarely took advantage of and after a month, he was running on fumes, just in time to return to work.

Not long after he returned to work, the station started to receive letters and emails from viewers that asked if Tom Hatcher was drunk. His investigative stories were turning bitter and his confrontations with deadbeat business owners and slick politicians were growing more venomous. He would often zone out for a brief moment during questioning only to return with a biting remark that not only stunned his subjects, but the audience as well. After his station manager was through reviewing a bitter interview one day, he pulled Tom aside into one of the empty editing rooms for a friendly chat.

"Hey, buddy, how you doing?" Gene Roberts asked. Gene was a throwback from the days of hard reporting. He held true to the saying that "if it bleeds, it leads" and he was known for his knack of letting anyone within earshot know exactly how he felt about any given situation. Many of the fresh faces at the station thought Gene was just a grumpy old man that was fighting retirement and the next generation of television reporting. Tom thought otherwise. To Tom, Gene was a breath of fresh air. When you spoke with Gene, you knew exactly where you stood and it was liberating, something that the younger reporters couldn't quite handle or understand.

"As good as expected, I guess," Tom said. His eyes were bloodshot and his face gaunt. It was ten times worse on camera and all the make-up in the world couldn't hide the hurt that was spreading through his veins like a poison with no antidote.

"Listen, I'm not going to pussyfoot around the problem. You're too good of a reporter, Tom." Gene placed his hands on his hips and took a second. "The stories lately, they've been..."

"They're good pieces, Gene."

"No, they're good subjects, Tom, but the reporting isn't."

Tom crossed his arms and appeared insulted, not because he was, but because he wanted Gene to think he still cared. The truth was, work had burned Tom out and he would have quit a long time ago if he could, but he needed the insurance.

"Come on, Gene. That councilman is a crook. I'm not going to softball questions to him."

"Jeez, Tom, I'm not asking you to ease up, but to be more tactful, for crying out loud. You bull over these subjects like your conducting the Nuremberg Trials."

Gene was angry, Tom could tell. He didn't like it when his reporters argued with him, even the ones he liked. No one just followed orders anymore, was a common gripe form

Gene. And he was right. Now everyone wanted a reason. It was a kinder and gentler corporate world and Gene hated it.

"Why don't you take some time to focus on the things that matter?"

"I don't have any vacation or personal days left."

"I know."

Tom frowned and looked Gene dead in the eye. "You firing me, Gene?"

"It's not like that. Your job will be here when you're ready. The station just can't sell the farm, you know. It's still a business, Tom. And, like you, I just work here. Not to mention, we've been getting phone calls and letters from viewers about your stories. It's not good for the image we're trying to uphold here."

"Viewers? Really? Now we're concerned about what the viewers think?"

Gene clenched his jaw and puffed out his

chest then said, "This station has always been concerned about our viewers. That's your stinkin' audience, Tom. But if that's not good enough for you, the sponsors are starting to hint that they don't like Mr. Tom Hatcher and you know as well as I do, that's bad news, pal. Corporate may not care what the viewers think, but they sure as hell care what the sponsors think."

"They said that?"

"In so many words"

"Who?"

"It doesn't matter, does it?"

Tom let out a sigh and his shoulders slouched. Gene was right. It didn't matter. Once the people that paid the bills started questioning if it was worth the money for advertisement, you were done. That was the way the world turned in corporate news. Tom knew that Gene was having mercy on him.

"I need the insurance, Gene."

"You'll still have your benefits. I just can't pay you. It's the best I can do."

"So, what? Laid off?"

"Administrative leave."

"Unemployment?"

Gene shook his head. "Can you do it?"

"Do I have a choice?"

"Not really."

Tom thought about it for a moment then said, "All right."

Gene relaxed. He patted Tom on the shoulder then said, "We're all here if you need us, Tom. And like I said, your job will be here when you're ready."

"I appreciate it. I really do."

Tom cried that night, muffling his sobbing with his pillow so Tiffany wouldn't hear him. Gene didn't fire him, but it felt like it.

Even though he would have quit if it were just him, he still had his pride. Tom was worried that after all that had happened, he was now going to let his career tank because he couldn't keep it together any longer.

He prayed a lot during those days, not knowing exactly what to say or what to expect, but he figured the tears and moans got his point across to the Almighty well enough. At first, the prayers were quick and to the point then they moved on to a lot of waiting. That was when the crying would come. He thought that the waiting would usher in some kind of response, but all he got in return was the beating of his own heart and the constant hum of his brain. It was lonely and despair often crept in, overcoming him, which threw him further into the murky waters of the abyss. He was depressed and he knew it, but he didn't know what to do about it.

As a child, he never went to church. His father didn't believe in God and what little his mother believed gave way to apathy. Tom and Sarah rarely attended a service, but for the occasional Easter Sunday or

Christmas Eve. After Tiffany was born, they stopped going even to those services, though Sarah always regretted it. Tom would reassure her that they didn't need to go to church to believe in God. Of course, he wasn't even sure if he believed regardless. The idea of a corporate body of people singing songs to the thin air and placing a guilt offering in the plate discouraged any longing for a real church experience, but life has a way of handing out beatings and soon options thin.

Tiffany began to have sore throats and fevers a few months after the surgery. Tom informed Doctor Mehta immediately and she moved one of Tiffany's CT scans up a few weeks to have a look. He sat across from Doctor Mehta in a common office used by doctors to discuss the good and the bad.

"My concern is that the cancer has metastasized and spread to Tiffany's lymph nodes," Doctor Mehta said. "However, an early diagnosis may prevent further spread, if that's the case."

"How will you know?"

"The CT scan showed some growth on her lymph nodes and I ordered a biopsy and blood tests."

Tom's head was spinning. He didn't know how much further he could go with the bad news piling on, one after the other.

"If it turns out that the cancer has spread, I suggest starting chemotherapy and radiation treatment immediately."

"Man," Tom said, shaking his head. He saw what chemotherapy did to his own mother years ago. The pain that she went through made her death seem like a relief in the end. He stood up, dazed and confused, then said, "What about surgery?"

"Chemotherapy is the best course of action, Mr. Hatcher."

Tom felt the bitterness growing within. It was bitterness toward cancer, toward life, toward God. But most of all, and the most heartbreaking for him, it was bitterness toward Sarah. It was her genes, her family, and her godforsaken immune system that had cursed their little girl with a looming death sentence. Death sentence? Stop thinking like that. It was more than he could bear. The cancer was heavy, but the hate... The idea of actually hating the love of his life after she had abandoned them so quickly poisoned his soul even further. Something had to give.

The growth on Tiffany's lymph nodes turned out to be cancerous and, as Doctor Mehta suggested, she started chemotherapy immediately. It had been two weeks of poisoning her young body to rid it of that death cell when Tom walked into the church on Sunday.

CHAPTER THREE

Tom gazed out the window slit of his jail cell. The parking lot was empty with a few sea gulls loitered about as dusk crept in. Michigan was beautiful during the spring and Tom realized he had not noticed the snow had melted and the trees were budded green. For the first time, he was really looking at was around him and he laughed to himself. There was a time when he looked forward to the changing of the seasons. Like chapters in a book, they brought new beginnings and expectations, but now they came and went, reminders that life changed whether he liked it or not.

He heard the click-clack of the cell door as it unlocked and it whined when it opened. Tom turned and saw a buzz cut officer holding a clipboard.

"You made bail. Let's go."

It took them twenty minutes to release Tom and give him his wallet, keys, belt, and cell phone. He signed some paperwork then they compared his face to his mug shot to insure that the Sheriff's Office did not accidentally release some maniac in his place. As the last door buzzed open, Tom saw the man he had cold-cocked that morning. He was holding two cups of coffee. Pastor Dan nodded to him.

"You've got to be kidding me," Tom said to himself and he walked out to meet Dan.

"By the way, my name is Dan Underwood," he said as he handed Tom a cup of coffee. "And I believe you owe me an apology."

A broad smile crossed Dan's face and Tom took the coffee, smirked then enjoyed a sip.

"You're right. I do and I'm sorry," Tom said.

"I forgive you. How about a lift home?"

Tom looked back at the steel door and the deputies working the desks inside the jail. Could someone refuse bail? Hitting the man was inexcusable, but a short ride in a car with him was not on the top of Tom's bucket list either. People like Dan were always working on some kind of angle, whether it was souls or building bigger churches. Tom was not in the mood to have his soul searched and he knew nothing about carpentry. Three hours alone in a cinder-block room with fluorescents buzzing overhead was enough of a deterrence to make him decide against knocking on the steel door and asking to be put back in the county hoosegow, however.

They drove in silence for a few miles before Dan decided to break the ice.

"You know, I used to watch that morning show you did."

Tom sipped his coffee and stared straight ahead. It was dark and there was no moon. He was not sure how to react to that statement, so he decided he wouldn't say anything. The county jail was only eight and a half miles from his home on Main Street. If he kept his mouth shut, he could get away with just a "thanks for the ride."

"It took me a bit to realize who you were," Dan said. "You look different in person. Course, you're not usually slugging people on TV." Dan looked over at Tom and smiled. Tom ignored him. "You're doing those ambush stories now, right?"

Tom wasn't sure what Dan Underwood was trying to do. Was he looking for a friend? Well, Tom didn't need a new friend. His coffee was too hot, so he lifted the lid to cool it down. A question deserved an answer. He sighed, looked into his coffee cup and saw his eyes reflected in its murky surface.

"Investigative reporting," Tom said.

"What's that?"

"I'm an investigative reporter. I don't ambush people."

Like most people, Pastor Dan did not
know Tom Hatcher, except for what he saw
on television now and then. Tom looked
over at Dan and he saw that he was studying
Tom, trying to get a read on him. No doubt,
Pastor Dan saw a guy trying to live each day
better than the last. At least he hoped.
Despite the anger and coldness, Tom was
just a man like everyone else. It was hard for
some people to humanize a person that was
on television. Tom had seen it before.
However, Dan Underwood knew better than
most that Tom was just a man like him when
he punched him in the nose in front of his
entire congregation. No, Pastor Dan was not
looking for a friend. He was looking to save
a soul.

"Haven't seen you for a while. Working on
an undercover story or something?"

Tom's instincts egged him on to tell the
man of God to go stick it and just take him
home. However, his instincts landed him in
jail for the first time in his life, too. If
anything this day had taught him, it was that
his instincts sucked.

"Administrative leave."

"Suspended?"

"Why would I be suspended?"

"Anger issues would be my guess."

"I don't have anger issues. Just a bad day. Like I said, I'm sorry I took it out on you."

Tom gave Dan a quick glance and noticed he was smiling at him. What was this guy smiling about? There was nothing pleasant about any of this. Tom was not amused. Why should he be? No matter how much Dan tried to lighten up the day's events, it all boiled down to everyone around Tom dying from a horrible disease and he couldn't handle it anymore. There was nothing even remotely amusing about any of it.

"Anything else?" Tom asked.

"I didn't mean anything by it."

They were on Main Street, just past Rudy's Market. Tom could see his house coming up on the left. It looked neglected, even though it was as immaculate as the rest of the surrounding homes. It looked that way to Tom ever since Sarah had left him and no matter how hard he worked around the house, it would never have the vibrancy it once had when she made it a home.

"That's me on the left. The blue one."

"I love these old homes," Dan said. "I always wondered what they looked like inside."

"Like a house." Tom couldn't wait to get out of the car.

Dan drove past the house and Tom craned his neck, watching it then said, "Are you kidnapping me?"

Dan laughed then said, "Your car is parked at the church."

"Oh, yeah." Just a few more miles, Tom thought.

Dan hit the accelerator as they pulled

away from downtown
  and the road opened up to four lanes.

  "Listen, Tom. Is it okay if I call you Tom?"

  "What else would you call me?"

  Dan chuckled and said, "You got me there.
Hey, regardless of everything that happened
this morning, I'm here if you need someone
to talk to. I mean it."

  "Well, that makes everything better,
doesn't it?"

  Tom instantly felt bad for the attitude, but
Pastor Dan wasn't catching on. God had his
chance. This morning was the final call.
Nothing matter now. He just wanted to go
home.

  Dan pulled into the church parking lot and
eased up alongside Tom's car. Tom quickly
opened the door and said, "Thanks for the
ride." Then he slammed the door shut.

  As he started his car, Tom thought how it
would be nice to talk to someone, but not a

preacher. He felt he couldn't get a straight answer from a Bible thumper anyway. Some heavenly perspective that would not be practical to Tom's situation would taint every bit of advice. Besides, God wasn't in the Tom Hatcher business. It was apparent that Tom was alone on this planet and it was up to him to get through life on his own, good or bad. He put the car in drive and pulled out of the parking lot.

CHAPTER FOUR

Tom drove his Buick Rendezvous down I-75. It was a 2005 model and it used to be Sarah's car. He bought it for her when they moved to Clarkston and presented it to her with the exclamation, "It's a brand new used car!" She laughed then hopped around the car clapping. She loved the Buick. After she died, Tom couldn't bring himself to get rid of it, despite the tell tale signs that it would need a new transmission soon. Whenever he stopped then took off again, the car jerked with a thud from underneath as if it were shifting into drive for the first time. He had the transmission flushed and the problem only seemed to get worse.

He was driving to the Detroit Children's Hospital located in the Wayne State

University district. Per Doctor Mehta's suggestion, Tom moved Tiffany there to gain access to the best care possible. He promised Tiffany that he would come down right after the church service. She asked him to tell Jesus to say hi to mommy. That was two promises he broke. The Beatles song "While My Guitar Gently Weeps" blared from the car's speaker system and he could feel every riff of Clapton's wailing guitar. It was his favorite Beatles song. He once saw George Harrison at the airport in Tampa and he yelled for him. George turned and smiled then waved and kept on his merry way. It was a high point for seventeen-year-old Tom Hatcher. He told that story for years, his close encounter with a Beatle, and he thought about it every time he heard the song. Of course, now Harrison was dead. Cancer. Tom couldn't even escape the grips of cancer in a song. He turned the radio off. Traffic was light so he bumped the gas and brought the car up to seventy-five miles per hour. The streetlights overhead trailed into his rear view mirror.

Tiffany was sleeping when he walked into her room. He sat in a chair by her bedside

and tried to read an old edition of Country
Home that he found in the waiting room.
The name on the address label was none
other than Sarah Hatcher and he
remembered that he donated a stack of her
old magazines to the hospital. He fell asleep
and only woke up once when a nurse came
in to draw blood from Tiffany. She slept
through it and the nurse quietly asked if she
could get him anything. He said he was fine
and he drifted back to sleep.

"Daddy. Daddy." The whispered
exclamations awoke Tom. He opened his
eyes. The room was bright with the morning
sun. Tiffany was sucking chocolate milk
from a straw and looking at him. He sat up,
his neck kinked from the odd angle in the
chair.

"Hey, baby girl. Good morning."

She smacked her lips as she sucked the last
of the chocolate milk from the carton. The
sun highlighted her thin light brown hair
and her hazel eyes were bright and wide.

"You were snoring." She made a sound

like a pig then giggled.

Tom smiled and wiped the sleep from his eyes. A cup of coffee, still steaming, was on the nightstand. He picked it up and took a drink.

"The nurse said that was for you."

"Was she pretty?"

"Dad? Yes."

"Good. Coffee is always better coming from a pretty girl."

"You're silly."

"How are you feeling?"

"Can I go home today?"

He knew the answer was no, but said maybe anyway. She asked if she could watch cartoons and he found Nickelodeon on the television. Only once did she ask where he was yesterday and Tom lied and said he was sick. She said, "Poor daddy" and rubbed her little hand through his hair. They watched every annoying cartoon, one after the other, and it made him miss Bugs Bunny and the Roadrunner something terrible and he thought that the kids today had no idea what they missed out on when it came to cartoons.

Later that morning, Doctor Mehta checked in and Tiffany asked how she was feeling and told Tom that things were looking well, but there was still some cause for concern as the tumors on her lymph nodes were not shrinking as fast as she had hoped. However, they were shrinking nonetheless. She then asked how he was doing and Tom lied again for the second time that day and said he was doing as well as expected. He could tell that she didn't believe him when she offered him a referral to a counselor. Tom reassured her that he was doing fine, the third lie.

Again, as he did with Dan Underwood, he thought that it would be nice to talk to someone, but it was not in him to do so. Hatcher men generally did not talk about their feelings to anyone. It was a miracle if they did. When Tom thought about it, he

could only remember one time when his dad
said he loved him and it was right before he
dropped dead from a massive heart attack in
the middle of the living room. Tom was
home from the University of Florida and
they were having an argument about
something that Tom could not recall. Tom
saved his most fiery dart for the end when
he told his father that he did not love him.
His dad stood up from his favorite easy
chair, pointed a bony finger right at Tom,
and told him that he loved him very much
and that everything he had ever done was to
show him and his mom how much he loved
them both. But it was pride that got the
better of Tom and instead of apologizing, he
stood and groaned disbelief then shoved his
father out of the way and tried to leave the
room.

His dad didn't make a sound. Tom heard
the thud when his body hit the floor. When
he turned to look, he was dead. His mother
tried for many years after to get him to shake
the guilt of that day. That is, until her own
terrible and slow death from cancer. On her
deathbed, she asked Tom one last time to
make it right with his dad, but it was too late

and he knew that he would carry that burden with him forever. Death canceled everything but memories.

He continued the no-talk tradition into his marriage. It was a source of aggravation for Sarah and she often erupted into a mountain of fury when Tom would sink back into himself and grow silent during an argument or "intense dialogue" as Sarah called it. They didn't argue often, and for the most part, their marriage was strife free, but there were always those moments. Of course, those moments were always a result of Tom not communicating. Sarah would always say, "You know for a guy in the communication business, you're lousy at it." To which Tom would reply, "I'm sorry, but I don't have a teleprompter for life, babe." That somehow always diffused the situation and Sarah would shake her head and suppress a smile then tell him, "I just want us to be better. That's all," and they would hug it out.

Once Tiffany arrived, he started to open up more, but only for the good things in life. He still wasn't comfortable dealing with the raw emotion of disappointment, sadness, or frustration. It embarrassed him and he didn't like the way it made him feel vulnerable. Sarah knew the buttons to push and she did so with glee sometimes. It used to drive Tom crazy, but now he would give anything to have those buttons pushed by her again.

Doctor Mehta had mercy on Tom and left, telling Tiffany that she would be back later in the day to look in on her. It was lunchtime and Tiffany wanted chicken nuggets from McDonald's, so Tom said he would go and get her some.

"And chocolate milk?" Tiffany asked.

"Okay, but you can't drink chocolate milk all day."

"Why not?"

"Cause it's not good for you."

"Dad, I'm in the hospital."

Tom smiled, kissed her on the cheek and left to get his insightful and wise beyond her years daughter some chicken nuggets and chocolate milk. Luckily, there was a McDonald's at the corner of Mack Avenue and Chrysler Drive, a mere half- mile from Children's Hospital. Outside of the restaurant, a vagrant, who smelled like cigarettes and urine, asked for five dollars. Tom gave him a buck and the guy barely grunted thanks as he sat back against the wall, scratched his matted beard, and waited for someone else to come by.

After driving around the hospital for five minutes looking for a parking space, Tom finally gritted his teeth and paid for parking in the garage next door. As he walked toward the entrance of the hospital, he noticed a young woman in purple scrubs sitting on a bench eating a sandwich. She was looking up at the cherry blossom tree next to the bench. He passed by her and she looked at him and smiled. Tom's heart did something and he smiled then mumbled profoundly, "Hi."

On the elevator ride to Tiffany's floor, he thought about the girl on the bench. He thought about how she held her sandwich with just her fingertips and when she took a bite, it was small and pleasant. Her eyes were green and her nose freckles. Her feet were small and they bobbed to a private beat. It must be the reporter in him, he thought. His attention to detail even impressed him. He caught a glimpse of himself in a brass plate on the elevator wall and saw something he hadn't seen in a while. He was smiling. Tom snorted, chuckled, and then said to himself, "You're an idiot." The elevator stopped. The doors opened. He delivered the goods to his little girl. She was more excited for chicken nuggets than a person should be.

They spent the afternoon playing Go Fish, watched television, and made up new words. Tiffany liked the word game, because as she said, "They can mean anything you want." Most of the time, the words meant something silly or defined a mythical creature she just made up. Other times, the words took a deeper meaning laced with innocence. Those moments often caught Tom off guard. Tiffany had a knack for profoundness without knowing.

At around three o'clock, a nurse came in.

She woke up Tiffany from her nap and said that it was time for her chemotherapy. Tiffany cried and begged her dad to let her skip one session, just this once. The nurse was all business. She reassured Tiffany that it would be over before she knew it. Tom listened to her whimper and cry as the nurse pushed Tiffany out of the room in a wheelchair. An hour and half later, Tiffany returned, sick and uncomfortable. She moaned in her bed until finally falling asleep. Tom kissed her. He placed his hand on her head and said, "Please." Then he went home for the evening to get some rest so he could be back early in the morning.

CHAPTER FIVE

The house was dark. Outside the wind picked up in gusts that slammed the siding and blasted sheets of rain against the windows. Flashes of lightning broke the darkness into jagged shadows in the bedroom. Tom fell asleep listening to the hum and creaks of the house and the rain outside and he dreamed.

He dreamed he was in a room with no doors. A small square window high and out of his reach was the only way to the outside world. The gray glow of the moon casting a shaft of light to the middle of the room broke up the darkness. Tom sat on a bench along the wall with the window. The bench went from corner to corner around the entire room. People sat beside him and all around.

Some were faceless, others were people that he knew, and yet there were more he did not know.

A man in a flowing robe, spotted with charred stains and holes with glowing embers burning in the darkness, stood at one side holding a tray with a loaf of bread. He stopped at each person and whispered to them and then they would tear off a piece of the loaf and eat it. Tom didn't know the man, but he knew his voice. The man made his way around the room, whispering and offering bread from his tray. When he stopped at Tom, he stood there, saying nothing, staring down at Tom.

Tom looked to either side of him at the faceless men. He heard them weeping. As the man in the robe bent toward him, Tom's heart thumped as if it were trying to escape the bony prison of his rib cage. He smelled the remnants of smoke coming from the man's robe.

Tom looked up to see the man, but he couldn't see his face then he heard him say, "Take and eat. Don't be afraid."

Tom's mouth was dry as he tried to wet his lips to say something. His tongue was think and callous. The man spoke again, telling Tom to take and eat and not to be afraid. But he was afraid and he didn't know why. The bread sat on the tray like an offering. He looked up at the square window. It was too high to reach. No escape. Trapped, his heart thumped harder.

From across the room, Tom saw his father. He was younger than he remembered and he waved then pointed the same bony finger he jabbed at Tom before he died. Tom turned to the men next to him and passed his hand before their empty faces. They didn't move, but they continued to weep. Then he heard her voice and it took his breath away.

A cold sweat broke out on Tom's brow and the more he wiped at it the more he would sweat. Her voice was like a whisper and it called out to him. He did not want to look, but he could not help it. Tom slowly turned his eyes upward to look deeper into the hidden face of the man wearing the robe and he saw Sarah. She smiled at him and Tom cried. The two faceless men beside him wept even louder. She reached out and touched Tom's face. He longed for her. Her fingers were warm and wet. He touched them and saw that they were dripping with blood. Tom pulled away.

"Shh, don't be afraid, darling," Sarah said. "Eat the bread. Everything will be okay."

He found no comfort in her words and his fear grew stronger. Tom's heart picked up the pounding rhythm he was sure would kill him and sweat trickled down his brow, down the bridge of his nose and dripped from the end of it. He tried to speak but only moaned. Everyone started to laugh. His fear turned to embarrassment then anger. Sarah pushed the bread toward him and smiled. Tom hesitated. His hand trembled as he raised it to reach out for the bread. He grabbed it and instead of tearing just a piece of the loaf, he took it all and devoured it in one bite. The bread was hard going down. He needed water. He couldn't breathe. He tried to stand. The two faceless men next to him held him back and their weeping turned into wails and moans. Their cries mixed with the laughter of all the others. Tom tried to pull away, but the faceless men were too strong. He looked up at Sarah and pleaded with his eyes. She smiled and watched. Her eyes were like that of a doll, black and innocent while cold and lifeless at the same time. Finally, with a jerk and a gulp, he forced the bread down his throat then screamed, "You're killing me!"

"To die is to live," Sarah said.

When he awoke, Tom was cold and the sweat had soaked through his pajama bottoms and into the sheets. He reached down to feel the dampness and realized that he actually wet the bed and he felt his face blush and he turned his head to Sarah's side to make sure she wasn't lying in the urine. It was empty, of course, and sadness and shame overcame him and he felt paralyzed as he lay in his own urine, staring back up at the ceiling. He missed her.

From a tree outside the window, a mourning dove cooed. It broke the silence in his head and his brain throbbed against his skull. His mouth was like a dry summer heat and Tom finally mustered the strength to swing his legs around and sit up. He peeled the wet pajama bottoms off and checked the time. It was six and for a brief moment there, he thought he could smell freshly baked bread.

Tom turned on the hot water and watched it go down the drain. It gurgled and choked as the water swirled around the drain and disappeared. His arms hurt, as if he had spent the day before lifting weights. A voice in his head said, "No pain, no gain" and he snickered, cupped a handful of hot water, and splashed it onto his face. Tom looked into the mirror and he said, "To die is to live."

On his drive to the hospital, all Tom could think about was the dream. Why had he been so afraid? Why was Sarah so determined that he eat the bread? Then there was the blood. Why was she bleeding? He told himself it was just a dream. It was just a bad dream.

He passed his exit and had to take the next, driving through downtown Detroit. The city was now a shadow of its glory days.

Like cancer, poverty had overcome and stolen the vibrant life of the city formerly known as the Jewel of the Midwest. Abandoned buildings were shadows on the streets and gated shops held vigil for customers that never came. People wandered the streets, their eyes tired and their souls vacant.

He pulled into the parking garage across from the hospital and paid the three dollars to park. It was eight o'clock and Tiffany was by now awake and wondering where her daddy was. He trotted across the street to the entrance and went inside.

The elevator door was closing and Tom yelled out, "Hold the door, please!"

He reached the elevator. The woman from the bench held the doors. She was in scrubs again, this time pink. She looked up at him and smiled and he smiled back and said thank you. The doors shut and the elevator began its climb.

"What floor?" she asked.

"Three. Thanks."

She pressed the button marked three. Tom looked at her I.D. badge and saw that her name was Melissa Nolan. He looked up and caught her eye then looked away. Her eyes were as green as remembered. Freckles covered her face, not just her nose. Her hair was red and he guessed her age to be thirty-something. He could smell lavender and his heart did that something again as she cleared her throat.

The elevator stopped at the third floor and when the doors opened Melissa said, "Have a nice day."

Tom stepped out and turned then went to say something, but he only managed a smile as he watched the doors shut.

Tiffany was up and she was upset. She was pouting. Her arms folded across her chest as she watched Tom enter the room. He stopped at the foot of her bed and placed his hands on his hips.

"What did I do?"

"How come you didn't sleep over?"

"I had to go home to change and shower. You don't want your old stinky dad hanging around here do you? People might talk."

She turned her head, showing her disapproval. "I don't care."

Tom walked around to the side of the bed and kissed her on her head then sat down.

"You say that now. Besides, I care."

She sat back with a thud against her pillow and grunted to make sure that Tom understood just how upset she really was. Tom acted as if he was going to stand.

"I can go back home, if you want?" Tiffany relaxed and her eyes widened. "No. Stay."

"All right, I'll stay," he said while sitting back against the chair. "Has the doctor been in to see you, yet?"

"Just a nurse."

"Was it the mean one or the nice one?"

Tiffany grinned and said, "You mean was she pretty?"

"Same thing."

"Daaaaaad. She was nice."

"Good. I told them I didn't want the cranky nurse to bother you anymore."

"No, you didn't!"

Tom smiled and said, "No, but I can if you want."

Tiffany smirked and gave her dad a suspicious look then said, "Daddy, I wanna go home."

"I know, honey, but they have to say it's okay. You want to get better, right?"

"Yes."

It killed him each time he had to tell her that she couldn't go home and judging by the look in her eyes, he guessed that it killed her a little, too. He reached out and took her small hand. He rubbed it. Her skin was soft.

"How you feeling today?"

"Good."

"Do you want to play a game?"

"No."

"Watch TV?"

"No."

"Then what? What do you want to do? Anything you want."

"I wanna go home."

Tom knew he wasn't going to get anywhere with her once she had fixated on going home. He sat back in his chair and grabbed the Country Home magazine from the table next to the bed. It was going to be a long morning.

By noon, Tiffany's mood had changed. They brought her favorite food to eat, macaroni and cheese with chocolate milk. The macaroni and cheese smelled like a foot, but it tasted great. Tiffany didn't want the applesauce that they gave her, so Tom ate it. It was bland. He washed it down with some old coffee he found in the waiting room down the hall. It was awful, but being the coffee addict Tom was, he didn't mind. He could drink a pot of joe from an old shoe if he had to. He loved the stuff.

After lunch, Doctor Mehta paid a visit and brought some good news to make it an even better afternoon.

"Tiffany is able to go home by the end of the week," Doctor Mehta said.

Tiffany squealed and hopped up and down in her hospital bed.

"That's great," Tom said.

"Of course, she'll continue her treatment in outpatient, but we'll no longer put her through radiation. That's a good thing."

That was the best news of all. The radiation had started to turn her skin red and her hair was thinning rapidly. That was the first thing Tiffany latched on to, as well.

"Will my hair grow back?" she asked.

"Eventually, yes," Doctor Mehta said.

"We could always get you a wig," Tom said.

Tiffany smirked and groaned then said, "Daddy, wigs are for old ladies."

Tom and Doctor Mehta laughed and Tiffany continued to hop up and down in her bed.

"The only downside, I'm afraid, is that you won't be able to go back to school just yet," Doctor Mehta said. "Her immune system is still too weak and the chances of her getting sick could make things complicated. It's important that she stay as healthy as possible while in treatment."

Tiffany stopped hopping and groaned her

disapproval.

"Hey, you're still going home," Tom said.

Tiffany thought about it for a second then smiled and said, "Yeah."

After Doctor Mehta left, Tom said that he was going to go outside for some fresh air. He wanted Tiffany to take a nap. She resisted, but he held his ground and told her that she wouldn't be able to watch television later if she didn't. He closed the drapes and turned out the lights then tucked her in and kissed her before going for his walk.

CHAPTER SIX

Melissa sat on the bench that she always sat on during her lunch hour under the blossoming cherry tree. She had made sitting on the bench a habit after she first spotted Tom Hatcher in the lobby of the hospital. She waited to see Tom walk by everyday for the last couple of weeks. Every day, he walked with his shoulders forward and his head down. It was contrary to his looks. He had the face of a confident man, lined with experience and forethought. Melissa could tell that he was hurting and she wanted to reach out to him. He didn't notice her for two weeks. Then yesterday he said hi to her and today they shared an elevator ride.

She knew him from television, of course. He was as handsome in person and she wanted to meet him. However, he never looked like he was in the mood to meet a fan. Most people in hospitals aren't in the mood to meet anyone.

She took a bite of her sandwich and heard the front entrance to the hospital slide open and she saw Tom Hatcher walk out. Her heart skipped a beat and Melissa crossed her legs and waited for him to walk by. She was nervous and looked back over at him standing at the front entrance. They made eye contact. She smiled. Tom returned her smile then he walked over to her.

"Hi," Tom said.

She cleared her throat and said, "Hello."

Tom looked up at the blossoms on the cherry tree. His shirt was open at the top and his neck looked strong. The blossoms moved in an easy breeze.

"I love the way the blossoms smell, don't you?" Melissa asked.

Tom sniffed the air around the tree and

she did the same. It was sweet, soft on the senses. The blossoms refreshed a warm spring day.

"You come out here often?" Tom asked.

"When it's warm," she lied.

He appeared nervous and he was making an effort not to look at her directly. She sat still, her body resting lightly against the green wood planks of the bench. Her eyes reflected the sunlight for him and the wind tossed her red hair gently around her freckled face. He was blushing. Was he trying to pick her up?

Melissa's nervousness grew. She took a small bite from her sandwich then a sip from her Diet Coke as she watched Tom Hatcher from the corner of her eye. He had lost weight, or it was true that the television added ten pounds. He had a chiseled face, but his eyes were tired. Tom Hatcher had big hands that looked strong and he occasionally bit his fingernails. Unlike most news people, he didn't keep his hair perfectly combed. It was nicely trimmed and held up well no matter how the wind blew it about, though.

"Um, you're Tom Hatcher, right?"

"The one and only."

He rolled his eyes. Melissa held back a smile.

"And you are…"

"Melissa… Nolan."

She reached out her hand and he shook it. He held her hand firm to let her know that he knew how to control himself.

"Nice to meet you," Tom said.

"You, uh, work here?"

"No. I just like to dress up like a nurse and hang out at hospitals. Next week, I'm going to try the police station."

Tom laughed. Melissa smiled. She was glad he got her humor. Most didn't. She scooted over to make room on the bench for him. He raised an eyebrow then took a seat next to her.

"Were you going to get lunch?" she asked.

"No, just some fresh air. Hospitals make me sick."

"I know the feeling."

Melissa reached in her lunch bag and pulled out an apple then offered it to Tom.

"You can have it, if you want. I never eat 'em. Always pack one, but never, not once, have I eaten it."

"It's not the same one, is it?"

"Could be. Not sure."

He took the apple and said thanks. Melissa realized that he was looking at her mouth.

"I have something in my teeth, don't I?"

Tom smiled and nodded then took a bite from the apple. "A piece of lettuce," he said.

Melissa picked the lettuce out of her teeth then turned to Tom with a wide grin and said, "Is it out?"

Tom looked close and nodded then tossed the apple in some bushes.

"It's bad, isn't it?"

"Worst apple ever."

"That makes me feel better about wasting them by the bushels."

"You buy them by the bushels."

"I think so." She laughed. "Actually, I don't even know what a bushel is."

"Too many."

"I just don't have any luck with apples. I can never pick a good one."

"Well, nobody's perfect."

They both laughed as the breeze picked up, swaying the cherry blossom overhead.

They sat on the bench trading witty banter and telling silly stories from work for the rest of Melissa's half hour lunch break. She never asked him about the little girl in the hospital room she saw him with one day while she was delivering x-rays. And he never offered to tell her about the little girl. It was a light-hearted moment for the both of them, a distraction from what went on inside Children's Hospital of Detroit. It wouldn't last long, though.

Tom sat there on the bench after Melissa had left to go back to work. A breeze came and showered petals from the cherry blossom tree overhead onto Tom. The sweetness of the blossoms surrounded him and he breathed in deep. Though Children's Hospital was crammed in the middle of the city, there was a certain kind of peacefulness to the surroundings. The hospital was off the beaten path of everyday city traffic, so the only vehicles that rumbled by were those that were driving to and from the hospital. The bench was a great place to just sit and think without distractions. No wonder Melissa often ate lunch there.

He wasn't thinking of anything particular.
Tom's mind jumped from one subject to the
next, from one face to the next. One minute
he would remember something that Melissa
said and the next he would remember
something Sarah said.

He thought about Tiffany laying in her
hospital bed and the next he imagined
Melissa coming in to talk to him. He thought
about making love to Sarah and then she
turned into Melissa. He was embarrassed.
The death of Sarah was still too near for him
and the clouds rolled in.

By the time Tom walked back into
Tiffany's room, he was an emotional mess.
The guilt of enjoying the company of another
woman weighed heavily on him. He didn't
even notice that Tiffany was awake. Tom sat
down in the chair next to the bed and closed
his eyes. As he fell asleep, he heard Tiffany
say something about heaven and an angel
and then he was out.

CHAPTER SEVEN

The sun broke through the clouds. It was Friday and Tiffany rode home with her dad and a bouquet of flowers that Doctor Mehta gave her. They were daisies. Tiffany told Doctor Mehta that the daisy was her favorite flower. She wore a surgical mask that covered her mouth and nose. She had to wear the mask whenever they were out and about until Doctor Mehta said that her immune system was strong enough not to. They listened to Disney Radio all the way home and Tiffany was so excited that she sang every song as loud as possible.

The house smelled like Windex and it was spotless. Tom had hired a cleaning service the day before to come in and scrub the house from top to bottom. Doctor Mehta suggested a good cleaning to help Tiffany ward off any germs that might be in the house.

Tiffany ran upstairs to her room and broke out her stuffed animals for an impromptu tea party as soon as they walked through the front door. Tom placed the daisies in a vase and set the vase on the table in the dining room. He heard Tiffany's voice and the ticking clock hanging in the kitchen. Joy and loneliness intertwined. It was good to have her home.

The day before, Tom and Melissa spent her lunch hour in the hospital's commissary. A storm raged outside.

She did most of the talking. Tom, for some reason, didn't have much to say. He felt he should have, though. Melissa talked about how she became a nurse and that she loved the satisfaction she got when she helped people. For years, Melissa worked in a doctor's office as a medical assistant. She spent her days taking care of appointments, battling insurance companies, and chasing payments. It was a thankless job, in her opinion, so she went back to school for her nursing degree. It was the best decision she ever made.

She was from Ann Arbor, that booming college town packed with rabid Wolverine fans. Her father was a retired political science professor and her mother an artist.

"What kind of art?" Tom asked.

"Folk art mainly," she said. "You know, Grandma Moses type paintings, quilts, wood thingamabobs."

"Wood thingamabobs?"

"I don't know. Mom never was one to talk about her work and I wasn't interested."

"Sounds like my relationship with my father."

"Don't get me wrong. She was a good mother. We just didn't have much in common. That's all."

"Have you ever been married?"

Melissa almost choked on her Diet Coke then said, "God, no.

Are you kidding? Never even had the time to look, what with school and now my job. What about you?"

"I was."

"Divorced?"

Tom tapped his finger that still held his wedding band. "Widower."

She wondered why she never noticed the ring before. To tell the truth, it hadn't dawned on Melissa even to look. For a moment there, she was appalled by the thought they she could have been, for lack of a better term, hitting on a married man. Then she wondered if what she was doing was hitting on Tom Hatcher. Of course she was. Why wouldn't she be? He was a handsome, eligible bachelor sitting across from her on a rainy Thursday afternoon. She would be a fool not to be.

"I'm sorry to hear that, Tom."

"It's almost two years now." She reached out and held his hand. "Our daughter has cancer."

Melissa liked the way his hand felt as she caressed his finger with her thumb. He looked down at her hand then into her eyes.

"I've never said it like that," he said.

"I'm sorry." She didn't know what else to say. What do you say to someone whose daughter is fighting for her life? Sometimes, Melissa took the sick for granted. It was her job to care for them, but like most things you do every day, it was common and ordinary. Sick people were just a part of life. Melissa felt lucky not to have death so close to home. It was merely a professional part of her life.

Tom's eyes drifted back to her hand on his and said, "Thanks."

That was it. He didn't go any further into the what, when, and how. He just left it at that. It was too soon for details. She didn't press on. It was none of her business, not yet, anyway. Not yet? What was she hoping would come from these lunch dates? Lunch dates? Were these dates? Melissa asked if he wanted to have lunch again tomorrow and he said yes without even thinking.

Tom stood in his living room looking at the bouquet of flowers and listening to Tiffany upstairs carrying on. He remembered their lunch date and looked at his watch. It was noon, and by now, Melissa was probably sitting on the bench wondering where he was. He had no way of calling her. They never exchanged numbers. He had to accept the fact that he was about to make someone very unhappy. Hopefully, she would understand.

At one o'clock, the phone rang. Tom was busy going over bills. He had worked on a crossword in the Oakland Press earlier, but avoided the news stories. He could not bring himself to think about work or to take notice of what stories he was missing. However, he could not bring himself to throw away the two weeks of unread newspapers stacked on the kitchen counter. It just felt wrong.

The phone rang a second time. Tom

finished writing out a check to the electrical company, a whopping $18.00, the benefit of rarely being at home, he guessed. He answered the phone and heard a disconcerted voice on the other end.

"Tom?"

"Melissa?"

"I looked you up in the database. I hope that's okay."

"Hey, I'm glad you called."

"Did you forget about our lunch?"

"I'm sorry. I did. Tiffany got to come home today and…"

"That's good news."

Tom felt like a heel. He held the phone away and sighed then said, "She's still in outpatient. Maybe we could do lunch or coffee when we're down there."

"That would be nice," Melissa said. "Just

let me know when you're coming down."

"It's a deal."

"Enjoy having your little one home."

"Thanks. You, too. I mean, thanks."

He heard her laugh on the other end then she said, "We'll talk soon."

"Wait! I don't have your number. That's why I didn't call you."

He heard her laugh again on the other end. It eased his guilt. She gave Tom her number and they said their goodbyes. That same feeling he had the first day they sat on the bench outside of the hospital came back. He went about paying the rest of his bills.

The next morning, Tom and Tiffany enjoyed a lazy day of morning cartoons, chocolate chip pancakes, bacon, and Go Fish. It wasn't much different from when she was in the hospital, except minus the constant interruptions from doctors and nurses or the occasional blood draw.

During lunch, they sat in the sun-room watching the geese waddle near the shoreline of Old Mill Pond. A swan cruised slowly by and a family of mallards walked up out of the water and started to pick at the grass in their yard.

"Daddy, can I go see the ducks?"

"Not today, honey. The doctor said you had to stay inside."

"But I feel better!"

"You can get sick. Not today."

"But..."

"Thems the rules until Doctor Mehta says differently."

Tiffany dropped her chin to her chest and said, "Yes, Daddy," then took small, pitiful bites from her grilled cheese sandwich.

Tom felt awful. It was unnatural for a child to just sit and do nothing. It wasn't in her to not go on some adventure. And the ducks, dear God, the ducks! How it ate at her adventuress spirit not to chase the ducks!

"You want to build a fort in the living room instead?" He said with as much excitement as possible.

A smile crept in as she took one last pitiful bite of her grilled cheese then she nodded.

"You do?"

Tiffany looked up at Tom with mischief in her eyes and said, "Yeeeesssss."

They spent the rest of the afternoon tearing the living room apart, building a fort out of the cushions from the couch, bed sheets from upstairs, and anything else that would do. Tiffany was the princess, of course, and Tom was a knight rescuing her from the ghastly dragon. In this case, the dragon was a stuffed lion aptly named Leo. He was very cooperative and took great delight in playing the part of the dragon, according to Tiffany.

They ate dinner under the cover of a bed

sheet and made up words. Afterward, Tom and Tiffany had ice cream sandwiches in the sun-room and watched the sun cast an orange hue across the gentle pond.

That night, as Tom tucked her in, he read her a story from a book he found on Sarah's bookshelf next to their bed. He had managed to clean out most of Sarah's things a few months after she died, but he could not bring himself to rid of the books she had collected by her bedside. Occasionally, Tom would pull one of her many romance novels out and read until he drifted off to sleep. He enjoyed them even though he made fun of her for reading them. She would have found it funny and ironic.

The book he chose to read for Tiffany was a Time Life book Sarah bought at a garage sale called, The Life Treasury of American Folklore. It was a book filled with American myths and legends. The story he read was Charles M. Skinner's How Sam Hart Beat the Devil. It was a short story about a man named Sam Hart. He outwitted Satan in a horse race. Tiffany liked it because it had horses and she had Tom read it three times.

Finally, after the third time, Tom said that it was enough and that she had to go to bed. He tucked her blanket around her tiny frame and kissed her cheek.

"Daddy?"

"Yes?"

"Why was Sam afraid?"

He supposed that Sam Hart was afraid because he didn't want to lose his horse and he told Tiffany as much. She didn't think that it was a good enough reason.

"He could always get another horse," she said.

"True," Tom said. He saw her wheels turning and he had to ask, "Why do you think Sam was afraid?"

Tiffany didn't answer right away. She had to be sure of her answer. She always had to be sure. Finally, she looked up at Tom and said, "Because he was scared to lose his soul?"

It was hard to believe this was a kindergartner, but Tom knew she was a young girl that had been through more in life than most adults had five times her age. He smiled and rubbed his hand across her thin head of hair.

"What do you know about losing your soul?"

"I dunno."

"Do you even know what a soul is?"

"What?"

"It's you. It's your spirit inside of you. The part that goes to heaven."

Tom watched her ponder the thought then she said, "So, he was afraid he wouldn't go to heaven?"

"I suppose."

"Is Mommy in heaven?"

"She's watching you right now."

"Can I go to heaven?"

The question was a dagger to the heart and a lump formed in Tom's throat. He took a second to control it then said, "Someday."

Tom leaned over and kissed her on her cheek again then said he loved her. As he left her room and turned out the light, he heard her whisper, "Dear Jesus," and he shut the door.

He dreamed that night. He was in the room with the benches, only this time he was alone. The room was dark. A television sat in the middle, casting a glow across the floor. The window was boarded shut. He smelled smoke and bread crumbs were at his feet.

Tom walked toward the television and knelt before it. The picture was of Sarah's funeral and he saw her mom and dad in the front row. Sarah's dad clapped and sang as Tiffany skipped in a circle in front of the casket. Dan Underwood stood at the podium and he was laughing. Tom reached out and touched the television screen and the static shocked him.

"It's not funny!" Tom shouted.

Dan Underwood laughed even harder and soon everyone joined him. Sarah's dad sang louder and clapped faster. Tiffany ran and skipped to the tempo. She was tired and started to cry. Tom grabbed the television by its sides and shook it.

"Stop it!" he cried.

Sarah's dad clapped even faster and Tiffany tried desperately to keep with the time.

"Make it stop, Daddy! Make it stop!"

Tom frantically switched the channel, each one revealing the same torturous show. He picked the television up and threw it across the room, smashing it to the ground, but it kept playing.

Tiffany ran until she eventual collapsed then the singing and clapping stopped. Everyone stood and looked down at her crumpled body.

Tom fell to his knees and cried out, "No! Please, God! No!" The television switched to the emergency broadcast system. Its tone overpowered his cry. Tom covered his ears and moaned, "Make it stop!" Then there was silence.

He lay on the floor and sobbed then he heard her voice. "To die is to live."

He looked up and saw Sarah standing next to the television. She wore her blue burial dress. Her pasty skin had too much blush to give the illusion of healthiness. Her feet were bare and dirty. Tom reached out to her and tried to say something. His voice didn't work, though. He grabbed her by her feet and sobbed until he couldn't breathe.

"Shh, don't be afraid," Sarah said, barely a whisper. "Don't be afraid."

When he awoke, Tom snatched the sheet off him to see if he had wet the bed again. The bed was dry and then he cried. He climbed out of the bed and stood then immediately fell to his knees and sobbed. Tom crawled to the door. He wanted to check on Tiffany. He felt weak and helpless. He reached for the doorknob. It wouldn't turn. He collapsed, hyperventilating and sobbing.

"Tiffany!" he cried out. "Tiffany!"

There was no response and he grew angry and started to thrash about, knocking over the nightstand next to his bed.

"Tiffaaaaaany!"

Then there was a squeak as the doorknob turned slowly. Tom watched it. He held his breath and waited. The door cracked open and beyond it was only darkness. He shook uncontrollably and he tried to scoot away. Then he heard her voice.

"Daddy?"

Tiffany opened the door wider and saw him lying on the floor.

"What happened?"

Tom sat up and reached for her, she ran to

his arms, and he squeezed her.

"Are you okay?" he asked.

"Yes."

She looked up at him, worry in her eyes. Tiffany started to cry.

"Why are you crying?" Tom asked.

"Because."

Tom squeezed her tighter and laughed. He felt stupid and sorry for scaring Tiffany.

"Daddy just had a bad dream and fell off the bed, but I'm okay now."

Her crying stopped and she sniffed and gulped air then said, "Was it the devil?"

He thought of the room and the television. He thought of Tiffany running in a circle as she cried. He thought of Dan Underwood laughing and he thought of Sarah in her blue dress and dirty feet. To die is to live.

"No, honey, it wasn't the devil."

CHAPTER EIGHT

It was Sunday morning, a week since Tom punched Pastor Dan Underwood in the nose before his entire congregation, and Tom was putting on his best tie while Tiffany changed dresses like politicians change their minds. She wanted to go to the church Tom went to last Sunday. He suggested a different church, but she insisted. He tried again, but she begged him, so he finally agreed. She was hard to resist when she batted her round eyes and her bottom lip pouted just so.

Tiffany barged into his room wearing a pink dress with green polka dots and shouted, "How 'bout this one?"

"Isn't that the first one you showed me?'

"That one was green with pink polka-dots and a pink ribbon."

"I think they all look great."

She gave Tom one of her Sarah looks, the kind that told him that he was out of his league. Sarah gave him those looks all the time and she was usually right.

"I'm going to wear the green one."

Tiffany ran out of the room and Tom tried to remember how to tie a Windsor knot then opted for the Half-Windsor instead.

During the ride to the church, Tiffany asked if she had to wear the surgical mask inside because it didn't really match the dress she was wearing. Tom looked over at Tiffany and thought that the pink Minnie Mouse ear hat wasn't helping, either. He told her that she had to wear the surgical mask and reminded her that she could not go into children's church. She had to sit with him in the adult service. She said it was okay and that she wanted to see the big service anyway. That was where the good stuff happened. Tom laughed and pulled the Buick into the church parking lot.

Inside, a couple wearing nametags that identified them as part of the church hospitality team greeted them. Their names were Donny and Marie. Tom stifled a laugh when he shook Donny's hand and as they walked away, Tiffany asked him what was so funny.

"Nothing," Tom said. "You wouldn't get it."

They stood in the middle of the church atrium. People crowded about and the mixture of perfume and after-shave dominated the faint aroma of coffee drifting from the rustic café near the entrance of the church. Tiffany looked up through the frosted glass suspended high above them. Posters of children from around the world garnished the walls and a metallic gray globe hung from wires halfway between the glass and the hardwood floor. The sunlight was a milky hue that lit up Tiffany's green dress with pink polka dots and shone brightly on her light skin.

"Daddy, look at how big that is!"

"It sure is."

An older couple smiled when they heard Tiffany's exclamation about the globe and Tom smiled back. Then they recognized him and gave him the stink eye.

"Long time, no see," Tom said.

The old woman shuddered and grunted her disapproval and the old man shrugged and followed her when she stomped away.

The worship band started to play from inside the sanctuary, or as the church called it, the Spiritual Life Center. Tom knew this by the etched stainless steel sign above the double doors leading inside. Everyone herded past the two women charged with handing out the Sunday morning service program, bottle necking at the door then blossoming into the Life Center. It was dark and the stage was aglow with theater lights and an abstract backdrop. The band worked its way up to a lively performance as people continued to find their seats in the crowded rows.

Tom and Tiffany walked in and he took a program from one of the women. Her jaw dropped and she turned to a nearby usher and whispered in his ear. The usher stabbed a look at Tom then spoke into a small transmitter that hung loosely from an earpiece much like the ones the Secret Service wore when they protected the President. Tom kept a suspicious eye on the usher, but tried to look harmless.

"What's wrong, Daddy?"

"Nothing. Let's find a seat."

They made it through one song before an usher asked to speak with Tom. Tom told Tiffany to stay in her seat and that he would be right back. Out in the hall, the usher introduced himself.

"I'm Mac..."

"Big Mac," Tom said. "Yeah, I remember you."

"And I remember you. I'm afraid I'm going to have to ask you to leave."

Tom laughed then said, "You're kidding, right?"

However, Big Mac was not smiling and he now had a couple of church thugs at his side. They were older men, probably grandfathers. They looked harmless, but were very serious.

"No, I'm not kidding. Get your things and leave."

It took a minute to register. Tom still thought that Big Mac was joking, but when he didn't break from the character of the man in charge, Tom suddenly found himself in an awkward situation. After all, why would they allow him back into the very church where he assaulted their pastor anyway? It was an appropriate response to him being there. However, Dan Underwood had also bailed him out of jail. He even told Tom that if he needed anyone to talk to, he was available. Then again, Tom told him to buzz off. But this was no way for a man of

God to react, even if it was by representation. A visitor had the right to worship. Wasn't this America? Tom narrowed his eyes. He thought about letting Big Mac have it. That wouldn't solve anything, though. He turned and started back for the Life Center. Big Mac grabbed him by the wrist.

"Where you going?"

Tom jerked his wrist free then said, "To get my daughter."

Tom entered the Life Center with a nervous usher in tow and went to the row where Tiffany stood on a chair clapping along to the music. The worship band cranked out a holy ballad and the people were convinced and invested in their worship. Tom grabbed Tiffany by her hand and pulled her down, practically dragging her away. She pulled back and Tom scooped her up and carried her out.

"Wait!" Tiffany said. "It just started!"

Some people turned to watch, but the

music was so loud that most of the people did not even notice Tom or hear Tiffany.

They burst out into the hallway where Big Mac and his holy goons were waiting. Tom stopped and glared at the men.

"These men say we can't stay, Tiff. They're making us leave."

Tiffany was crying now and said, "Why? That's not fair."

"No, it's not," Tom said. "It's not fair at all."

"Look, don't make this a bigger deal than it has to be," Big Mac said. He looked anxious. A crying little girl has a way of doing that to you.

Tom burned a look at Big Mac and said, "Where's your heart, man?"

Big Mac looked like he had more to say, but not the right words. He stared back at Tom with a blank expression that seemed cold.

"I'm sorry," he said. "You have to go."

"You got a lot to learn about people."

Tom then carried Tiffany out of the church as she cried and said over again, "It's not fair. It's not fair."

Tiffany cried all the way home and she cried, though it was a whimper by then, as she walked up the stairs to her room then she cried herself to sleep. Tom sat in the kitchen and stared at the clock ticking the seconds away. He was fuming and playing the scene over again in his mind. He wished he had refused to leave. He wished he had caused a scene again. He wished.

By late afternoon, five forty-three to be exact, Tom was playing with the idea of packing it all up and moving someplace where no one knew him or Tiffany. It was a silly fantasy, but it made him feel better to imagine that somewhere life was fresh and beautiful. They could start a completely new life together where she would not be the little girl with cancer and he would not be the burned out reporter from TV that punched a preacher on a Sunday morning. However, Tiffany did have cancer and would have cancer no matter where they settled down. Her doctor was here and her doctor cared. The feeling of being absolutely and utterly alone crept in again. Tom stood up, grabbed the ticking clock, and slammed it on the ground, breaking it into pieces.

CHAPTER NINE

Monday was a busy day for the hospital. It seemed that they scheduled everyone for their CAT scans, MRIs, and chemotherapy sessions on a Monday. Tom hoped that they could get in before their scheduled time and arrived an hour early. Two hours later, a nurse finally called Tiffany in for her treatment. Tom was not a happy camper.

He sat alone in a lounge on the main floor doing a USA Today crossword that someone left behind. As per his usual, he avoided actually reading any news articles. While he tried to figure out a five-letter word for brighter than bright, he heard Melissa's familiar laugh from the hallway. Tom looked and saw her talking to another woman in blue scrubs. Melissa held a clipboard close to her chest and she wore green scrubs this time. They were a bright, lime green and not the dark, depressing kind. She wore her hair in a ponytail and she tossed her head back with each laugh. Tom raised the newspaper to hide his face when he thought she would look in his direction.

He didn't Melissa to let her know that he was at the hospital. He was also not in the mood for conversation thanks to the two-hour wait. Melissa was nice and had a good heart, so it seemed. Tom was grumpy and had no heart, so it seemed. Besides, what woman in her right mind would want to get involved with a widower who had a child on the very brink of death anyway? Death? He wanted to stop thinking like that, but caught himself doing it more and more. He was sure that he made the right decision not calling her.

"Tom?"

Tom's heart sank. He lowered the newspaper and faked a smile.

"Oh, hi."

She looked at him with a mixture of joy and confusion at the same time. Tom stood and offered her an awkward hug. They found themselves caught between a hug and weird shoulder dance. Tom stood back and tucked the crossword under his arm.

"How are you?" Tom asked.

"I thought we were going to get together when you came down."

"Yeah, it was a last minute thing for Tiff."

He was a bad liar. Tom knew that she knew the hospital scheduled these things well in advance. He could see it in her eyes, too. She was hurt, probably confused, and probably angry, as well. He didn't blame her. Melissa straightened herself up and became a friendly nurse rather than a forgotten lunch date.

"Well, I hope everything goes well."

She turned to walk away, but Tom stopped her. "Melissa? I'm sorry. I wasn't really up to… anything."

"It's okay, Tom. If you don't want to have lunch with me, it's okay."

"No. I do. I do want to have lunch with you."

She gave him a suspicious look. Tom felt stupid and he looked around to see if anyone was watching. No one cared, but he still felt the embarrassment of everyone knowing that Tom Hatcher was a jerk, even if it was just in his own mind.

"I understand. Really."

Tom checked his watch then said, "Tiff is going to be out in a few..."

He couldn't read her face. It was blank. Sarah used to do the same thing. She would distance herself from what was happening in the moment physically, but emotionally, inside, she was boiling. It was only a matter of time before the pressure built and she exploded. Tom always tried to defuse the situation by pressing on. It never worked. It just made things worse.

"Are you upset?"

"No, don't be silly," Melissa said. "We can do it another time."

Tom shoved his hands into his pockets and looked at his feet. He thought his shoes looked worn. They needed a good polish. He shook of the thought then looked back up at Melissa. She was waiting for something, but Tom was thickheaded when it came to reading the signs. Some things never changed.

"I hope you're not mad," he said.

"Tom, I'm fine."

He nodded and felt a little better, though he couldn't be sure if it was all right.

"You do want to do it another time, right?" Melissa finally asked.

"Yeah. Yeah, of course I do." Then Tom had an idea. "How about dinner?"

Melissa smiled. He thought she smiled too

much. He may have jumped the gun.

"You don't have to," he said.

"No! That sounds great. When?"

Now he was committed. Tom said, "Tuesday at seven good for you?"

"That would be nice."

"Anywhere particular?"

"You tell me."

"How about Peabody's on Woodward?" Tom said. It was Sarah's favorite restaurant and the first one that came to mind.

"Never been there. Sounds like a plan."

"Okay then. Tuesday at seven. Meet you there?"

"It's a date."

She touched his arm lightly then walked out of the lounge. He watched her walk

down the hall then she turned the corner, out
of sight. It was too much too soon. He
should have just been honest with Melissa.
He should have told her that ever since
Sarah died, he was having a hard time
getting close to anyone, let alone another
woman. He had reserved his intimacy for
only two people for so long that it felt
intrusive and disloyal to offer it to anyone
else. Dinner was a bad idea. He was in no
shape to date anyone. The timing was all
wrong. Tom was having buyer's remorse in
the worst way and he felt panicked. He still
had Tiffany. She needed all of his attention.
It was all he had strength to do. His little girl
was knocking on heaven's door and he
needed to be there for her. Death again.
Knocking on heaven's door. Tom cursed
himself for his kneejerk thoughts. His panic
turned to guilt then to anger. Melissa should
have already understood. It was her fault for
making him feel that way.

Doctor Mehta came down to the lounge. A
nurse's assistant pushed Tiffany in a
wheelchair. Tiffany looked tired, but showed
no signs of being sick. Doctor Mehta told
Tom that she would probably not feel well

by the time they got home. He asked how she thought her treatment was going and Doctor Mehta said that it was going well. She would know more after Tiffany's next CT scan. Again, Doctor Mehta asked how Tom was doing and he assured her that everything was fine. Then Tiffany spoke.

"Who was that lady you were talking to, Daddy?"

Tom didn't think she saw Melissa and he didn't want to lie, but he didn't want her to think that he was picking up chicks while she was in treatment either.

"She's a nurse."

"She's pretty," Tiffany said.

"I suppose she is, Tiff."

"I bet she's nice."

"She was very nice."

Doctor Mehta pursed her lips in an attempt to suppress a smile. She raised her eyebrows and shrugged then said, "I'll see you next week?"

"Next week. See you then, doc."

Tiffany vomited once on the way home. Tom pulled over in the parking lot of the Oakland Mall while Tiffany hung her head outside of the window, crying and vomiting. He reminded himself to bring a paper bag next time then asked if she was all right. She whimpered and curled up in the backseat then slept the rest of the way home.

Tom pulled into the driveway. He got out of the car and went around to Tiffany's side. She was still sleeping and he picked her up and carried her up the steps to the front door. He fished for his house key and saw a piece of paper wedged into the door frame. Tom unlocked the door, letting the paper fall to the ground. He ignored it and took Tiffany upstairs to her bedroom where he laid her on her bed.

He went back downstairs and opened the front door to fetch the piece of paper. It was a note from Dan Underwood.

Hi Tom,

Stopped by to see you. I heard what happened Sunday morning. Please call me.

Dan Underwood

He wrote his number below his name. Tom reread the note a few times, trying to read between the lines. There really wasn't anything to read, but he did anyway. He wasn't sure he wanted to talk to Dan. He wanted to forget the whole incident. It was over with and there was no reason to keep poking at it. He didn't throw the note away, though. Instead, Tom stuck it on the refrigerator with an Elvis magnet that Sarah bought when they went to Graceland on their honeymoon. He looked at the magnet, remembering that crazy freewheeling week when they couldn't take their hands off each other.

Tom went into the living room. He pulled their wedding album out and flipped the pages to the honeymoon section. She kept the memories organized and entertaining. Sarah was big into the whole scrap-booking craze. It wasn't enough just to have your photographs stuck in album. They needed decoration and witty introductions.

On the page marked "Honeymoon," there was a self-portrait of Tom and Sarah in front of the Welcome to Graceland sign. They were young, babies really, probably too young to marry. The people in the picture did not seem like Tom and Sarah. Tom was thin in the face and Sarah's impish smile and wide eyes seemed almost unreal. They had their whole life ahead of them. Tom had graduated from Florida University with a degree in journalism and Sarah worked at an art gallery. They had no money, but they had a vision of a bright and long future together.

They went to Graceland, the home of Elvis Presley, on a whim. Driving through Tennessee, they literally came to a crossroad on their way to Chicago. Sarah's parents gave them a three-night stay in downtown Chicago as a wedding gift. Tom pulled the car over to look at the map and he started to laugh.

"What's so funny?" Sarah asked.

"Well, we could go north and get to Chicago two days early," Tom said. "Or we could take a detour to Memphis for a day."

"What's in Memphis?"

"Wanna go to Elvis' house?"

A devilish smile crossed Sarah's face and her eyes lit up. She shook her head and laughed as she curled her legs up against her chest.

"Ohhh, the King of Rock-n-Roll!"

"That's right, baby," Tom said in his best Elvis voice.

Sarah leaned over and kissed him then said, "You can do whatever you want."

"Hoochie mama."

Tom threw the car into drive and took the exit to Memphis, Tennessee. They spent a day filled with Elvis impersonators, a gaudy house, and ridiculous souvenirs. Tom did an impromptu Elvis impersonation in one of the gift shops that resulted in a spatter of applause and an extremely embarrassed Sarah. They ate lunch on Beale Street and listened to street musicians' belt out the delta blues on their pawnshop guitars and ancient harmonicas. Later that night, they slept in a one star motel near the airport and giggled helplessly as they listened to the deep southern couple next door argue over who was going to go to the store for more beer. Sarah slept in her clothes and Tom spent the night killing spiders and cockroaches. They never had such a good time.

Tom was asleep on the couch with the picture of the two of them in front of the Graceland sign in his hand. Whoever was knocking on the door had been doing so for a long time. The knocking was growing impatient.

The house was dark and Tom flipped on a table lap before getting up from the couch. He saw the silhouette of a man through the glass at the front door. He knew who it was before he even opened it.

"Hey, Tom. I saw your car in the driveway

and I thought I would stop to say hi."

It was Dan Underwood. He tried to appear casual. Tom hid a yawn then said, "What time is it?"

"It's nine-thirty. I'm sorry, did I wake you?"

"It's all right. Come in... I guess."

Dan entered and looked around. It was dark, but for the table lamp in the living room, and he saw a narrow and steep staircase leading up. The wood floor creaked as he went to remove his shoes, a habit in his house.

"You don't have to take them off," Tom said. "Anything to drink?"

Dan walked into the living room and sat on an antique rocking chair. The living room looked like a time capsule from the early nineteenth century, as if it came with the house.

"Water would be nice."

Tom disappeared into the kitchen. Dan looked up at the family picture resting on the mantel of the fireplace. Tom entered with a glass of ice water and handed it to Dan, noticing him looking at the portrait. He sat down on the couch.

"Thanks," Dan said.

Tom feigned a smile and stared at Dan. Dan took a sip of his ice water. Tom waited.

"I wanted to stop by because during a leadership meeting, today, I was told that you came to church on Sunday."

"It was a brief visit."

"I heard that, too."

Dan took another sip of water and shifted in his seat. The rocking chair creaked and snapped. Tom stared at Dan.

"I, uh, I want you to know that I talked to Mac. He's sorry for what happened. I'm afraid he's just a little overzealous sometimes."

"What kind of church are you running over there, Reverend?"

"You can call me Dan."

"Okay. What kind of church are you running, Dan?"

Dan took a sip of his water then held it in his lap. He took his time answering. "I hope that I am running a church that cares for their community and for one another."

"You got some work to do."

Tom could tell that Dan was nervous and shaking. His leg shook and now and then he would place his hand on his knee and stop. Dan set the glass of ice water on the hardwood floor next to his chair.

"Tom, I'm sorry for what happened on Sunday. It shouldn't have. It's my fault."

Tom sat back against the couch. He was not in the mood to argue.

"It's okay," Tom said then he heard the

creak of the stairs.

"Daddy?"

Tiffany crept down the stairs. She shuffled out into the living room with a stuffed horse cradled in her arms. She stood next to the couch and looked at Dan with her wide hazel eyes.

"Hey, baby," Tom said. "Come here."

He scooped her up onto his lap and held her. She kept a watchful and bashful eye on Dan. Dan smiled and gave her a little wave.

"Who's that?" Tiffany whispered.

"This is Pastor Dan," Tom said. "From the church."

She looked at Dan thoughtfully for a second then scooted off Tom's lap and approached him.

"Hi," Dan said. Tiffany held up her horse for Dan to see. "Is that your horse?"

"His name is Licky, 'cause he likes to lick people."

She pretended to have Licky slobber Dan and he laughed. Tiffany jumped back into Tom's lap and buried her head into his shoulder then peeked out to see Dan smiling.

"What's your name?" Dan asked.

"Tiffany."

"That's a beautiful name. How old are you?"

"Six and a half. Almost seven."

"Wow! Almost seven. That's pretty old."

Tiffany smiled then said, "Not really."

Tom kissed her on her head then lifted her off his lap, planting her feet on the floor.

"Why don't you go and get yourself some chocolate milk while Pastor Dan and I talk."

"Okay!"

She ran into the kitchen as Tom and Dan watched her disappear around the corner.

"She's a cute little girl," Dan said. "Cancer?"

Tom nodded then scooted to the edge of the couch.

"I'm sorry," Dan said. "The hair. I just figured…"

Tom looked up at the family picture on the mantel and remembered that there was once joy in this house and that it seemed so long ago.

"Listen, Dan, I don't want to waste your time here."

"It's not a waste."

"I appreciate you coming by, but..." he sighed heavily. "Tell Big Mac I said all is forgiven."

Dan picked his water glass off the floor and finished it. He stood then said, "I will. Thanks for the water."

He handed the glass to Tom then walked to the front door. Tom followed him. Before he opened the door, Dan turned to face Tom.

"I really am sorry for what happened and I'd like to invite you back. You know, for a second chance."

"Thanks, but no thanks."

Dan nodded then opened the door.

"You know, our lives are nothing but second chances," he said. "If you change your mind, we have a mid-week service on Wednesday at six forty-five. Love to see you there."

"Have a good night."

Tom shut the door and went back into the living room. He watched Tiffany guzzle the glass of chocolate milk. Despite the cancer and all of the treatments that went with it, her appetite was full. She smacked her lips and placed the glass on the kitchen table then ran off.

"You forgot to rinse your glass."

She scurried back into the kitchen and put the glass in the sink then ran upstairs.

"Still didn't rinse it," he said to himself.

Headlights lit up the room and crossed over the family picture. Tom took it off the mantel and rubbed his hand across Sarah's face.

"To die is to live," he said softly.

Dan had a short drive home. He didn't live far from the church, which was only two miles from Tom's front door. As he drove, he thought about his own life. He tried to think of Tom, but empathy was a powerful force that often chose its own line of thought.

Cresting over a hill, away from the lights of downtown Clarkston, Dan looked ahead into the darkness. Spots of porch lights broke up the night. Headlights headed in the opposite direction, toward Dan, not far in the distance. We trust people every day. We trust them with our lives and the lives of our loved ones. The highways test that trust each day. Dan thought about that trust and he thought about betrayal.

He took a slow and deep breath then exhaled. The headlights passed and Dan watched the taillights disappear over the hill in his rearview mirror. What did he know about forgiveness? What did he know about salvation? Dan felt unqualified with both, but felt that God was with him, too. He was just a man trying to find his way through life like everyone else. He was working out his own salvation and forgiveness. And God approved.

He smiled to himself and silently thanked the Father then said aloud, "Lord, bless that family and allow me to speak into Tom's life." He meant it more than he had ever meant any prayer in his life. It made him remember all of the times and missed chances he had in speaking into the lives of those that needed it most. Life was full of regrets.

"No regrets, Father," Dan said as he drove into the night.

CHAPTER TEN

On Tuesday morning, Tom and Tiffany were in the hospital again. She was running a fever and had a small cough. It happened overnight and it frustrated Tom. Despite the surgical mask and the constant cleaning of the house, her immune system was just too weak.

Doctor Mehta admitted Tiffany as a precaution. Tom raised his voice, saying that the hospital should have never released her in the first place. Cancer was having its way with his emotions and overall mental well-being. He hated the hospital, but they needed it and he hated that he needed it. Everything about the place raked on Tom's nerves. The bright florescent lights, the smell of antiseptic in the air, the constant low hum of murmuring voices and machines, and the everyday reminder of death lingering about was enough to drive any man crazy, and Tom was that any man. Doctor Mehta took the verbal beating with grace and told him that if he needed anything, to let her know.

After filling out various paperwork and signing unending forms for insurance, Tom finally left the hospital. Tiffany was asleep in her room. A nurse told him that she needed her rest and that they would look after her. He felt guilty, but he had to get out of there.

Tom stopped at the studio before driving home. When he walked in, everyone glanced in his general direction then quickly looked away. He didn't blame them. After all, what do you say to a man whose whole life was unraveling before your very eyes? Normally, you turn on a camera and capture the unraveling. Thankfully, it hadn't dawned on anyone to run a story on Tom Hatcher. At least, if it did, no one brought it up. That was probably a good thing.

As he stood at his desk, Tom tried to remember exactly why he had stopped at the studio in the first place. The only thing he kept in his desk was some pictures, a planner, business cards, and pads of paper. He certainly didn't need any of it. Maybe it was a habit. He was near downtown. He drove to the studio everyday for two years. He just forgot where he was going.

Tom felt a tap on his shoulder and he turned around to see Gene grinning. The old man must have seen him standing there looking like a zombie.

"You look lost, pal."

"I think I forgot why I was here."

"Was it to work?"

Tom faked a smile and said, "I'm always working."

Gene laughed that raspy guffaw that bordered on patronizing and put his arm around Tom. "I'm glad you stopped by. Have something I'd like to discuss with you. Coffee?"

"Yeah, sure."

They walked over to a kitchenette, Gene with his arm around Tom's shoulders. People nodded hello to Tom, and Gene waved for the both of them. He poured two paper cups of coffee and handed one to Tom.

"Cream or sugar?"

"No thanks."

"Ah, cowboy style. A man after my own heart."

Gene sipped his coffee, keeping an eye on Tom. Tom offered him a half smile and sipped his coffee, still too hot to enjoy. Gene was a nice guy, but always had an angle. Tom hoped that he would just get to the point.

"So, what do you wanna talk to me about, Gene?"

Gene sipped his coffee again then made a sour face and set the cup on the counter.

"Tom, the station would like to have some kind of idea of when you plan on coming back."

"Are you kidding? You're the one who put me on administrative leave. Now you want to know when I'm coming back." Tom sipped his coffee, agreed with Gene's facial critique of the swill, but it was black and it was strong. "Am I in danger of losing my job, Gene?"

It was probably best to come right out with it. Tom liked to know where he stood with people and situations. It's the reason Tiffany's illness drove him to the brinks of insanity. He had no idea where he stood and where all this was going. At least work was somewhat manageable and predictable.

"God forbid, no, Tom." Gene held out his hands and leaned back as if holding back an angry crowd. He knew how to play the part of an over-concerned friend and at the same time, a station manager who would go to bat for his reporters. "Corporate is only covering its options."

"What does that mean? I don't know what…"

"It means that they want to put someone in the investigative reporter role until you come back, but they don't want to make that transition if you're coming back any time soon. That's all."

"It sounds a lot like, 'Hey, we want to replace you, but don't want to get sued.'"

"It's not like that."

"Gene, you said that I would have my job here waiting for me when I returned."

"And it will be." Gene smiled and pointed at Tom, again bordering on patronizing. "It's just temporary, pal."

Tom leaned against the counter. He swirled the coffee around in the paper cup. The station was replacing him and Gene was covering for corporate. It was his job. That was why they paid him the big bucks. The temporary garbage that Gene was spouting was nuts and he knew it. Tom was on his way to pounding the pavement for man on the street comments at carnivals. He should have never agreed to take the time off. But what choice did he have?

"I don't like it, Gene. I don't like one bit."

"Look, don't worry about it. I promise when you come back that your job will be here. Take all the time you need."

"If you say so," Tom said. What else was there? With Tiffany back in the hospital, he couldn't even entertain the idea of returning to work. Something was going to give. Tom hoped it was his career. It was the lesser evil of the two options.

It was dusk when Tom pulled into his driveway. He turned the car off and sat there in silence. The house looked ominous. It was dark and he felt like if he went inside, he would never come out again and it frightened him. He was tired of being afraid of losing his career, afraid of losing his daughter, afraid of losing his mind. Everything was slipping through his fingers. The entire drive home, he kept going over in his mind the idea of being unemployed and having a sick daughter whose treatments did not fall on the cheap side of the world of medicine. The house glared down at him, its windows uninviting, warning him. He gripped the steering wheel and flexed his jaw. Tom tried to will the fear away. It wouldn't go. He started the car then quickly backed out and headed anywhere.

Tom drove through the streets of Clarkston then on to the nearby town of Waterford. He drove through the lakeside neighborhoods and could see through the windows families sitting down for their evening supper. At one house, an old man stood motionless in the middle of his yard, gripping a rake. He watched Tom drive slowly. Tom could clearly see every line drawn on the man's face. He imagined each line was a result of years of unspoken tragedy, one after the other. The old man's eyes were hollow and his mouth turned down with a stiff upper lip. He wore a hat that didn't quite fit and his clothes were two sizes too big. The old man was alone. No, he wasn't alone, Tom thought. He was lonely. Is that where all of this is leading?

The old man gave a half-hearted wave. Tom turned away and gunned engine as a family of ducks crossed in front of him. He stomped on the brakes. The tires screeched and he jerked ahead, hitting the steering wheel with his forehead. He shook it off and put the car in reverse then slowly backed up then stopped. Tom put the car in park and quickly opened the door and climbed out.

"Oh, God. Please."

Tom rushed around to the front of the car. The headlights skimmed the road and surrounding yards. The duck and her ducklings waddled back and forth at the edge of the old man's yard. She was quacking loudly and the ducklings were chirping. Lying in the yellow light of the Buick's headlights were two ducklings. They were dead. A guttural sob burst from Tom. He coughed and tried to hold it back, but it was too much. The damn had broken and the waters were rushing into the valley. Tom reached down and picked up one of the ducklings. He sobbed and mumbled words only he understood. The duck quacked and waddled in the yard. Tom looked up at it.

Tears streamed down his face.

"I'm sorry. I'm so sorry. Please forgive me. Please."

He saw the old man move toward him and he set the duckling down, stood up and backed away from it. The old man stopped at the edge of his yard. The ducks waddled a safe distance, but kept a close eye on the dead ones. The old man stared blankly at Tom. He held his rake as if he needed it to help him stand upright. Tom looked at him.

"I'm sorry."

He got in his car, slammed it into drive, and sped away. The old man waved in his rearview mirror.

Moments turned to hours and Tom found himself in the parking lot of a small Irish pub. It seemed like a good time to have a drink, so he parked the car and went inside. Three scotches and one badly burnt bar burger later, Tom was feeling numb. A Red Wings game played silently on a twenty-year-old television set propped up in the

corner of the bar. The joint smelled of stale
beer, popcorn, fried meat, and the stench of
barroom sweat. Aside from a few Guinness
mirrors and a shamrock or two, there was
nothing particularly Irish about the pub. As
far as places to go, the Tavern was at the
bottom of the list. Those that graced it with
their presence were the type you crossed the
street to avoid. The bartender, her name was
Stacy, had probably been a good looking gal
at one point in time, but those days had gone
with a vengeance.

Tom ordered another scotch. One more for
the road, he told himself. Stacy poured and
delivered with a yellow-toothed grin. Tom
fished in his pocket for some cash, peeled a
twenty off, put it on the bar, and said thanks.
Buried in his money was the note from Dan.
He studied it for a moment.

"Anytime? Okay, pal," Tom said.

"What's that, honey," said Stacy as she
brought back his change.

"Thanks for the drink. Keep the change."

"Thanks, sweetie." Stacy slipped the cash into her back pocket then went about the business of pouring another beer for a half-dead looking man at the end of the bar.

Tom pulled out his cell phone and dialed the number on the note. It rang three times before Dan answered.

"This is Dan."

Tom listened, but he didn't say anything. He didn't know what to say and he was a little embarrassed now. He realized that he had just called a preacher because he was drunk.

"Hello?"

"Dan Underwood?"

"This is."

Tom took a swig of his scotch then said, "It's Tom Hatcher."

"Hi, Tom. What's up?"

Tom thought he sounded a little too excited to hear from him and he polished off his drink before going on.

"Well, I'm drunk," he said with a hint of pride.

There was silence on the other end then Tom heard Dan cover up the phone and talk to someone then he came back on.

"Where are you?"

"At a bar."

"Which bar?'

"The Tavern."

"I know where it is. You need a ride? I can come and get you."

Maybe this guy was for real, or maybe he was just playing savior. It didn't matter, because Tom needed a ride and he was light on friends. The cabs in North Oakland County were pretty much non-existent, so he had to depend on the kindness of a stranger, though he and Dan were hardly strangers anymore.

"You allowed to come to places like this?"

He heard Dan chuckle then he said, "I think I can get the church to make an exception."

Tom ordered another drink. One for the road, he again told himself. Another two drinks in him and Dan finally walked in. He sat down beside him.

"Rough week?" Dan asked.

Tom let loose a sarcastic sigh, chuckled, and took a sip from his scotch.

"Have a drink with me."

Dan ordered a coke and Stacy delivered it in a spotted plastic cup. He thanked her and decided against actually taking a drink. He looked around the bar, at the plain faces and the empty souls.

"When's the last time you were in a joint

like this?" Tom asked.

"It's been many years. And to be honest, I was a little hesitant to come here."

"Why did you?"

"I remember a story when I was in seminary about a priest that used to set up shop in a pub in England. I think it was late 19th century. I think."

"Simpler times," Tom said and he took a drink of his scotch.

"Hardly. But anyway, the priest called his meetings Beer Sermons. He figured it was easier to go where the sinners were than to get them to come to him. So, here I am."

"I'm a sinner?"

"We've all fallen short of the glory of God."

"Speak for yourself. I'm the very essence of the glory of God."

Tom raised his glass in a toast then drained it. The ice cubes rattled in the glass as he slammed it on the bar.

"Stacy! Thank you for the hospitality." Tom stood. He was seeing double. He slapped Dan on the shoulder and staggered to the door then turned around and said, "Let's get outta here."

Stacy said he still owed for the last drink. Dan stood and pulled out a ten-dollar bill and put it on the bar.

"Does that cover it?"

"You want your change?"

"Keep it."

"Couple of big tippers like you two can come back anytime," she said as Dan walked out of the Tavern.

They rode in silence for a few miles. Tom rested his head on his hand and stared out the window. He watched the streetlights pass. They glared to the back of his eyes and he blinked each one away. The smell of scotch filled the car. It wasn't until they were heading north on Dixie Highway that Tom broke the silence.

"I'm not a bad guy, you know."

"I know."

"No, I mean it."

Dan gave him a serious look and said, "Yeah, I know. Everyone enters the crossroads of life in their own way."

"Crossroads," Tom snorted.

"It's not how they get there that's important. It's how they leave."

They turned onto M-15 and headed into downtown Clarkston. The moon was big and orange and peeked out behind the heavy oak trees that watched over the homes lining the street. When they passed the old town church, now bar and grill, Tom heard Dan say a silent prayer, asking God to bless the building. He looked back at Dan then sat up straight and watched his house come into view.

Dan pulled the car into Tom's driveway. Tom sat there, looking at the darkened home, its ominous shadow returning the fear he felt earlier in the night. He thought that as long as he stayed in the car, he would be all right. Dan waited for Tom get out, but after a few moments, he put the car in park.

"I want to help you, Tom. What can I do?"

"Nothing," Tom said, barely a whisper.

"You know life does goes on."

"Is that what the Bible says?"

"No, Robert Frost or the Beatles. Whichever you prefer."

Tom rubbed his face, trying to wipe away the drunkenness.
Dan watched Tom return his gaze back to the house.

"How did you lose your wife?"

Tom shook his head then locked eyes with Dan. He never told Dan that Sarah was dead. Dan must have seen the confusion in his eyes.

"She is dead, right?"

"Yes."

"I'm not a wizard. It's your house. There are no flowers planted outside and the weather has been outstanding. My wife's been keeping the local nursery in business all week. I think we have more flowers than beds. Plus, the other day, you never mentioned her and I never saw her, but you keep a family portrait above the fireplace."

"Could have been divorced," Tom said.

"I don't know many divorced men that keep pictures of their exes on the mantel."

"Maybe we're good friends. Maybe we want a normal childhood for our daughter. Maybe I'm still in love with her, but she won't have me back." He didn't know why he was arguing. She was dead. Why was he

152

insulted by Dan's deductions? He was drunk and that stupid house sat heavy in the night, watching him. He glared up at the house.

"Maybe," Dan said. "But she's dead, right?"

"Yeah, she's dead." Tom was still agitated.

"How did you lose her?"

The only people he had ever talked about Sarah's death with was her parents, Doctor Mehta, and, of course, Tiffany. The funeral home didn't count. They offered grief counseling, a service that the island called Tom Hatcher refused. His co- workers didn't know what to say. Few people do and he didn't hold it against them for it. He liked it better that way. Or, at least, he thought.

"Cancer. Almost two years now."

"I'm sorry to hear that."

"You and me both."

"What was her name?"

"Sarah."

"It's piling on, isn't it?"

Tom wiped the tears welling up in his eyes. "Sometimes."

"You know I've had many arguments with God over the travesty of cancer."

"Yeah, well, get in line, pal."

Dan nodded then put his hand on Tom's shoulder. Tears rolled down Tom's cheeks.

"I understand, Tom. The pain..."

Tom looked at Dan. "Nobody understands."

He opened the car door and stepped out then said, "Thanks for the ride."

Tom shut the door and staggered up the steps and into the house. The headlights from Dan's car lit up the house for a second and he heard the engine wind as he drove away. Tom steadied himself at the foot of the stairs. His mouth was dry. He went into the kitchen for a glass of water. He opened the cupboard and grabbed a bottle of aspirin, popped the top and shook two tablets out then swallowed them. Tom turned the faucet on cold and cupped water with his hand and drank. It felt good going down and it settled his scotch filled stomach.

As he walked through the living room, he dried his hands on his pants. The phone sitting on the table behind the couch was blinking red. He had a message and panic took over. Tom picked up the phone, dialed his voicemail, and listened. His heart was thumping. The first three messages were hang-ups and he erased them until he got to the fourth. It was Melissa.

"It's eight o'clock and I'm leaving Peabody's, so if you're on your way, forget it. I understand you're under a lot of pressure, Tom, but that's no excuse to treat people, me, this way." There was a pause and Tom could hear the traffic running along Woodward Avenue. Then she said, "This is probably stupid, but I'm going to say it anyway. I like you, Tom. I had hoped that

you liked me. Life is too short, you know?"
She paused again then came back. "I'm sorry
about that. I didn't mean... I hope
everything is all right." The message ended
and Tom clicked the phone dead.

He thought about calling her and
apologizing. He checked the time. It was too
late. She was angry and she had the right to
be. He had forgotten their date and he felt
bad. He wondered if he had done it on
purpose. He didn't really want to go on a
date anyway. No, the hospital and work,
they made him forget. He has too much on
his mind. Everyone does, Tom, he thought.
He should feel bad about standing her up.
He did. He would call her in the morning
and apologize. He would tell her everything
that was going on so that she would have a
better understanding. If she really did like
him, she would wait until things were better.
What if this was as good as it gets? He
gritted his teeth for thinking that. Of course,
it'll get better. It has to.

It was two-thirty in the morning and Tom
was sitting on his bed staring at the only gun
he had ever owned for over an hour. The

double-barrel shotgun that his grandfather
gave him when he was a boy leaned against
the wall in the corner by the dresser.

The day before, he pulled it out of the
closet and cleaned it. He didn't know why.
Tom had not touched or even thought about
the shotgun since the day they unpacked it
and he stored it in the closet the day they
moved into the house. It just seemed like a
thing to do. It was something to keep his
mind occupied.

After he finished cleaning and oiling the
gun, he hesitated putting it back into its sock
and back into the closet. Tom stood in the
middle of the room and gripped the
shotgun. He watched his knuckles turn
white for what seemed like forever. The
weight of it felt good in his hands. He began
to study the polish on the barrels, the
scrollwork on the stock. Tom pulled the
hammers back and snapped the triggers and
the shotgun clicked. He turned the shotgun
so he could look down the barrels, dark and
unending; promising to end whatever they
pleased; whatever he pleased. Finally, he
placed it in the corner where it sat there now,

whispering to him. It was whispering to him.
He could hear it. End whatever you please.

Tom pressed his hands against his head
and squeezed the thought. He groaned and
sat back against the headboard of the bed.
The shotgun's whispers faded just as he
drifted into a drunken slumber.

Just a few miles away, Dan Underwood
had his own thoughts to workout. Unlike
Tom, he wasn't drunk or in despair. He
wasn't thinking about suicide. Instead, he
was pondering the goodness of God. It was
something he did every night while the
house was quiet and everyone was asleep.
He sat in his study with nothing but his
thoughts and the Bible. It was a bookend to
his day. First thing in the morning was set
aside for his devotions. He would read a
psalm and a chapter from Proverbs then
reflect on them, a meditation of sorts. Then
Dan would pray and ask God to help him
make a difference and to strengthen the
church, his family, his conviction.

At night though, it was much different. He
rarely read the Bible before bed. He just liked

to hold it in his hands. It gave him comfort and he felt wiser for having it near. Instead, he thought about the day. He thought about the people he met and the conversations he had. This wasn't about church management. That was time between bookends. No, this was about self-management. This wasn't a time to ask God for favor, but it was a time to thank him for the blessings in his life. Usually, he thanked God for his family, for the church, for his health, for helping him overcoming an obstacle. However, tonight, he wanted to thank God for something entirely new, entirely different.

Dan wept as he thanked God for the gift in his life. He thanked God for Tom Hatcher, for helping him understand. He understood better than anyone did now. He wept, but his tears were tears of joy. For the first time since he had accepted Jesus Christ as his savior, he knew the reason for all of his suffering and pain. He knew that everything led to the crossroads and standing there with him was Tom Hatcher. He was there to help him choose the right road, a road of redemption. He longed for the responsibility, something that allowed him to step away from the comforts of Sunday morning preaching and altar calls to an audience that was willing and able. This was what it was all about and not since he made the decision to go to Bible College had God's spirit challenged him. He knew that this was a life changer for him and Tom. His faith would grow stronger, making Dan a better leader and pastor, and Tom would know grace that so few had a chance to realize in a real and practical way. It was a good end to the day despite the sorrow and hopelessness of Tom Hatcher and tomorrow would be so much better.

CHAPTER ELEVEN

It was six o'clock in the morning and Tom's head felt like the Fourth of July. He stood in the kitchen staring at the toaster, dazed from last night's bender. The first thing he did when he woke up was to put his grandfather's shotgun in the rafters of the garage. He couldn't risk another incident like last night.

The coffee stopped brewing and he poured himself a cup. Tom was tempted to add a little Irish to his black brew to take the edge off his hangover, but the very thought of it made him sick. He held his mug close to his nose and breathed in the warmth. It was dark roast and he loved the smell of fresh brewed coffee. There was a knock at the door before he could take his first sip of the morning.

Tom opened the door and Dan stood there. "I came to take you to church."

Tom sipped his coffee and said, "It's Wednesday."

"Prayer meeting."

"I don't think so."

"Come on. Some of our most dedicated members meet every Wednesday at eight to pray for the needs of others. It'll be good for you. I promise."

"Sorry."

"Don't you think you at least owe me for last night?"

"Guilt? The church never disappoints."

"I'm not leaving until you say yes."

He didn't want to go, but at the same time, he did, though he didn't know why.

However, he did need to get to the hospital. Tiffany needed him.

"It only lasts an hour," Dan said.

"There's coffee in the kitchen. I'll go get dressed."

They were at the church long before anyone. Dan invited Tom upstairs to the office where there was more coffee. The office area was clean with a conference room surrounded by glass in the middle. A leather couch sat outside some private offices and Tom took a seat.

"No, come on in my office. I have to follow-up on some emails and junk."

Dan's office was small, considering he was the head honcho. His desk sat diagonally across a corner of the room. Two chairs were before it and a pair of bookshelves lined the walls behind them. Everything was close together. It was big enough for three, but squeeze in a fourth and you start to sweat. A can of spinach sat next to a miniature sculpture of what looked like a glass man

shedding skin made of bronze. Tom picked
up the spinach and turned to Dan.

"Saving this for a special occasion?"

Dan chuckled and said, "Reminds me of
Popeye."

Tom smirked and set the spinach back on
the shelf then ran his finger across the
sculpture.

"The spinach reminds me that I yam what
I yam and that's all that I yam." Then in his
best Popeye voice Dan said, "And I can'ts
stands it."

That got a brief snort of amusement from
Tom then Dan's voice took on a more serious
tone.

"The sculpture reminds me that God can
change it. It's called 'Born Again.' Dean
Kermit Allison sculpted it. Heard of him?"

Tom held the sculpture in his hands,
turning it, and inspecting it. "No, I haven't."

The glass soul was not shedding the skin, but was bursting from it. Tom placed the sculpture back on the shelf next to the can of spinach.

At a half-hour before eight, the two of them went downstairs to the Spiritual Life Center. There was a dozen or so people seated near the front. Tom chose a seat in the back row, the same seat he sat in the morning he decked Dan in the nose. It was a subconscious decision. A few people came up to him and shook his hand. They smiled and said good morning before suddenly realizing who he was. To their credit, they didn't withdraw their hands or make a snide remark. They only looked curiously at him then walked away. Big Mac, the burly usher that sat on him then tossed Tom out the second time, was there. He made an deliberate effort to walk over to Tom and apologized.

"You didn't know," Tom said.

"I'm sorry anyway," Big Mac answered. "That's no way to behave."

"Hey, at least you never decked a preacher," Tom said with a smile. Big Mac grinned and nodded then he walked back to the front to join the others.

During the prayer service, each person took a turn praying for an individual or the church as a whole. Dan handed out cards on which people wrote their prayer requests before they started. Tom didn't participate. He only watched.

At one point, Dan took charge. He announced that same exclamation from Sunday that God cared and worked miracles. Tom felt the pit in his stomach again. Only this time, he didn't stand and demand answers. He knew there weren't any answers. It was just life. But he wanted to give Dan a chance. He didn't know why. He figured if it was so important for Dan to show up on his doorstep early in the morning just so he could bring him to a prayer service, the least he could do was sit through it.

Dan broke the prayer chain that was going around and said that he wanted to share something that God had placed on his heart.

"God has been working on me lately with regards to faith. We all have faith, whether great or small. And our faith is something that we need to nurture everyday of our lives if we are to grow in it. Faith is more about the daily issues of life than the big issues of life," he said. "Jesus instructed us when talking about prayer, to ask God to give us today our daily bread. We don't ask God to fill our pantry for the week, but we ask him to feed us daily through our prayers and the reading of his word. This establishes a powerful dependency on God. Without prayer, you cannot have faith. And without faith, you cannot pray. And faith comes by the hearing of the word."

Tom's mind began to wander. He yawned. He was bored and started think about Tiffany. He wondered how she was doing. Tom check his watch. It was 8:30. She would be up by now, probably eating breakfast. I bet she's mad that I'm not there. I shouldn't be here. I should be with her. Tom checked his watch again. Still 8:30.

Tom pulled his cell phone out to check for any calls. He turned the ringer off out of respect. There were no missed calls. There was no service, either. It was 8:31 now and he started to feel guilty for not going to the hospital the first thing in the morning.

He stood up and Dan balked in his moment of sharing as he watched Tom hurry out the door. Dan checked his watch then recovered.

"Bread is more than a daily staple to fill our bellies," Dan said. "It's a symbol of God's provision in life. It's food for the body, food for the mind, food for the fellowship of man, and, ultimately, food for the soul."

Tom stood out in the parking lot. He held his phone up, desperate for service. One bar. Two bars. No bars. One bar. He stood still, the phone held up, waiting. No messages. A cool breeze blew against his face and he remembered that he didn't drive to the church. He only lived two miles away, but the walk was over hills and down a busy road. Hitchhiking was not an option. These days, only maniacs and morons hitchhiked.

He turned and looked back at the doors leading into the church then back out to the parking lot then remembered he didn't have his car anyway. It was in the parking lot of the Tavern. Tom tilted his head up toward heaven as the breeze picked up in a gust.

"What do you want from me?"

The breeze calmed and there was only stillness. Tom could hear the sound of traffic from the highway and the sun broke through a cloud just enough to warm his face. It was a feeling of peace that washed over him. It was only temporary, an imagination. Tom took in a deep breath then exhaled some of the weight off his shoulders. He then went back inside.

He waited in the café, a rustic and comfortable corner near the entrance of the church for the remainder of the prayer service and was still there when Dan came out to see him.

"I want you to take me to my car."

"What's wrong?"

"Just take me to my car, please."

As they pulled out of the parking lot and onto the main road, Tom turned to Dan and said, "Why are you doing this?"

"Because, I can."

"I don't need any more friends."

"I just might be the only friend you have."
"
I got plenty."

"And yet you called me, last night."

Tom looked at Dan. Dan raised his eyebrows and smiled. Tom thought he looked like one of those sad clowns. He also realized that Dan Underwood was right. For the rest of the drive to the Tavern, he told Dan everything. He told him how he and Sarah met, about college, and about Florida and how much they both hated the lack of urgency that people had in the Sunshine State. He told Dan about Sarah giving birth to Tiffany and how it was after doctors told them she couldn't have children. Tiffany was their miracle baby. He told Dan about how he landed the job in Detroit, that he and Sarah were excited about starting a new life in Clarkston. They loved the All-American feel of the tiny village. He told him about his in- laws, about the silly songs Sarah's father sang, how Tiffany laughed until she peed. He told him about the headaches and the day he took Sarah to the hospital. He told Dan what Doctor Mehta told him, that Sarah had cancer while Tiffany slept on a vinyl couch in the waiting room. He wept as he shared the final moments of Sarah's life and how Tiffany cried and beg God to bring back her mommy. He told him about the doctors and nurses crying and how they could not enter the room to do their jobs after she had passed. He told Dan about how he and Tiffany tried to pick up the pieces and that he cried on the steps of Clarkston Elementary on her first day of school. He talked about how horrible Thanksgiving was, but that Christmas was wonderful when they surprised Sarah's parents in Florida. He talked about how everything had started to return to normal and that he and Tiffany were finally looking forward to the days ahead.

Dan listened. He never said a word. As he pulled into the parking lot of the Tavern, he turned to Tom and said, "Life is a flowerbed, isn't it?"

Tom knew exactly what he meant and he chuckled. Life was a flowerbed. It was beautiful to look at from a distance, even from a few feet, but if you got close enough, you could see all of the crap mixed in with the dirt.

Tom reached over and shook Dan's hand, much to Dan's surprise. "Thanks for the ride."

He opened the door and got out. Before driving off, he waved to Dan and he waved back.

CHAPTER TWELVE

Tom drove faster than he should have down I-75. He was listening to the oldies channel on the radio. Led Zeppelin always made him drive fast. It felt good to unload and he thought he was stupid for not taking the funeral home up on their counseling services when Sarah died. He knew now what a world of difference it would have made for him and Tiffany. Sarah would have been proud, too. He felt a tinge of hope as he took the exit to Children's Hospital. He and Tiffany would get through this and they would be all right. He just knew it.

On the elevator ride up to the Tiffany's floor, he caught himself whistling and he laughed. It had been a long time since he whistled. He used to like whistling. How could he have been so ignorant? That moment of unloading had worked a miracle. He actually had some pep in his step.

The elevator doors opened and he stepped out. He switched the tune he was whistling. He walked through the double doors and down the hallway to Tiffany's room. Tom poked his head in and saw that it was empty. No worries. They were always shuffling patients in this place. He strolled over to the nurse's station and asked a nurse who was ready for retirement, "Excuse me, but I'm looking for Tiffany Hatcher."

The nurse peered over her reading glasses and cocked an eyebrow. "Mr. Hatcher?" she said. "We've been trying to get a hold of you."

Tom pulled his cell phone out and checked for missed calls. There was none.

"I don't have any missed calls."

"Well, we've left several messages at your home."

Now he was worried. Why several messages? Where was Tiffany?

"At my home? Are you kidding? Who's the supervisor?"

"Mr. Hatcher, your daughter…"

"Where's Tiffany?"

"Tiffany is in the ICU. She had a seizure early this morning. We had to move her."

"Seizure?"

Tom's knees buckled and he braced himself on the counter. His mouth filled with saliva and a metallic taste rushed in. He felt his throat tighten then he vomited all over the counter and collapsed on the ground.

The nurse jumped back out of her chair and yelled something that Tom could not hear as the blood rushed to his head. The last thing he saw before he blacked out was a doctor shining a light into his eyes.

With a gasp, Tom awoke. He was lying on

a hospital bed. A heart monitor next to him was rapidly chiming and a nurse rushed into the room. He was drenched with sweat and he sat up in the bed. The bright florescent light overhead burned his eyes.

"Mr. Hatcher?" asked the nurse.

Tom tried to climb out of the bed. The nurse held him back and told him that it was all right. She yelled for help and a couple of nurse's assistants rushed in and held him down.

"I gotta get out of here!" Tom yelled.

"Mr. Hatcher, you're in the hospital," the nurse said. "It's all
right. Calm down."

Tom struggled against the grip of the assistants, his entire body tense and straining with every movement. He didn't feel the shot, but he felt the effects and slowly he relaxed then there was only darkness.

When he awoke for the second time, hours later, four to be precise, he had a splitting

headache and his mouth was like the bottom
of a rock quarry. Tom fumbled for the
nurse's call button and pressed it.

Like she had done a million times before,
the nurse walked in with a cup of water and
two pills. She handed them to Tom without a
word and stood by while he swallowed the
pills and drank the water.

He handed the cup back to the nurse and
said, "What was that?"

She smiled then said softly, "Tylenol.
Feeling better?"

Tom shrugged and thought it was a stupid
question. Didn't she just bring him a couple
of Tylenol? He looked at his arms and saw
an IV.

"It's just to keep you hydrated," said the
nurse. "No drugs."

"What happened?"

"Before you freaked out and had to be
sedated?"

Tom rubbed his head then said, "Yeah."

"You vomited all over the nurse's station then fainted."

He vaguely remembered doing something like that, but he wasn't sure.

"Sorry about that," Tom said.

"It's okay," she said. "We see all kinds of things here, believe me. It was no big deal, but you did give us a scare."

It was suddenly coming back to him. The nurse at the station told him that Tiffany was in the intensive care unit.

"My daughter?"

"The doctor will give you a quick checkup then you can go to her."

"How is she? What happened?"

"You can talk to the doctor when she comes in."

The nurse walked out. It frustrated him when the nurses told him that he could talk to the doctor. They knew just as much about Tiffany's condition, if not more, but hospital etiquette demanded that the doctors be the ones to spill the beans. It was good for the nurses. They didn't have to bear bad news. It was bad for the patients or family members that were desperate for information, though. The doctors in these places were often like Sasquatch. You heard rumors of their existence, but rarely saw one. Then there was Doctor Mehta.

She came in to see Tom. Of all the doctors, she was the most comforting and the most familiar. It was unfortunate that they had to know each other under the circumstances, but he was glad for it. Sarah would have liked her. She looked over his chart then smiled.

"Well," she said, "I think you'll be just fine."

"Not exactly your area of concern is it?" Tom said.

"I told them I'd check up on you. You know, keep it in the family." She winked at Tom and smiled.

"I appreciate it."

"The nurse will take your IV out and then you can go see Tiffany."

"Thanks."

She smiled again then placed her hand on his arm. "Tiffany isn't doing so well, Tom."

She called him Tom. She had never done that before. It wasn't a good thing when you daughter's doctor called you by your first name. It meant you were spending too much time at the hospital. It also meant that you were about to hear something horrible.

"Tell me," Tom said.

"We found lesions on her spinal cord. We're determining what we can do for her at this stage."

"What does that mean, at this stage?"

"At this stage of her treatment."

He tried to hold it back, but it suddenly released like a broken dam and Tom started sobbing. Doctor Mehta stood there looking down at him. He continued to cry.

"I'll have the nurse come in now," she said then left.

It took twelve grueling minutes for the nurse to return and just in time, too. Tom was entertaining the idea of ripping the IV out himself. As soon as it was out, Tom was on his feet, dressed, and out the door. The nurse insisted that he sign some paperwork and he told her that she could find him in the ICU if it was that important.

Tom splashed cold water on this face and looked in the mirror. His eyes were red and his face blotched. He let out a heavy sigh then dried his face with a paper towel and stepped out into the hallway of the intensive care unit. The nurse at the desk pointed him to room 601.

Tiffany had every tube the hospital had to

offer hooked to her. She had a breathing tube down her throat. Her tiny chest jerked up and down as the machine did the breathing for her. He sat next to her bed and held her hand. Tom rubbed his thumb across her soft knuckles.

"Daddy's here, Tiff."

Her chest raised and lowered as the machine did all the work. Tom rested his head on her bedside and listened to the machine.

"Please, don't take her. Let it be me. I'll go. I'll do whatever you want me to do. Just…"

He looked up at her little face. He could see Sarah in her, and it made him wish he had never been born.

CHAPTER THIRTEEN

It had been three days and Tom was
disheveled and incoherent. He smelled, too.
Doctors and nurses came and went; they told
him things, but that was all they were –
things. He didn't have a clue anymore. On
the third day, Doctor Mehta had mercy on
him and told Tom that he should eat,
shower, and rest. She emphasized the
shower part. She also prescribed some
sleeping pills to help overcome the anxiety
that was keeping him up. He didn't intend
on leaving Tiffany's bedside. He told Doctor
Mehta as much. She suggested that he at
least use one of the hospital's shower rooms
and get something to eat. Tom took the hint.

When he returned from the cafeteria,
freshly bathed, but still dragging, they had

removed Tiffany's breathing tube and she was awake, although, just barely. Tom rushed to her side and held her hand.

"Hey, baby girl," he said. "How are you?"

She tilted her head and gave him a groggy stare. Tom rubbed her thin head of hair and smiled. Tiffany offered a weak one in return. He talked to her for a little while, but he could see her eyes were heavy. He sang one of grandpa's silly songs and she smiled as she fell asleep. A few minutes later, Doctor Mehta entered.

"Tom, I have some things to discuss."

Tom kissed Tiffany on her forehead and walked out into the hallway with Doctor Mehta. He saw in her eyes that what she wanted to talk about was not a good thing. Doctor Mehta was a fine doctor, but her emotions often betrayed her. Tom braced himself.

"Feel better?" she asked.

"I do. Thanks."

Doctor Mehta fumbled through Tiffany's chart. She was having trouble with what she wanted to say. Tears started to well up in her eyes and drop onto the chart. Tom's chest tightened.

"Just tell me."

She looked up at Tom, the tears streaming down her cheeks. Her lip quivered.

"Tom," she hesitated then, "The scans came back with growths on her brain."

She gasped and tried to hold back a sob. She looked shocked and she placed her hand on her chest. Tom reached out and put his hand on her shoulder.

"My God," was all Tom could bring himself say. Then Doctor Mehta buried her head into Tom's chest and started to cry. Tom embraced her. The tears rolled down his face and, again, all he could say was, "My God. My God."

She finally stepped away and apologized for her behavior then told Tom that they would do whatever they could to help Tiffany. Tom thanked her and watched her walk away.

He wiped away the tears, blew out some nervousness, and walked back into the room. Tiffany was still sleeping. She probably would be for some time with the drugs they had given her. He sat down and watched her breathe on her own until he too finally fell asleep.

Six hours had passed. He rubbed the sleep away and stretched as he sat up in the chair. The room was dark, but for some moonlight through the blinds on the window. He saw that Tiffany was awake. She stared at the ceiling. Tom reached out and took hold of her hand.

"Tiff, honey?" he said.

She continued to stare at the ceiling. Tom squeezed her hand then kissed it. He looked up at his little girl. She had been crying only moments ago.

"Tiff, you okay? Do you need anything?"

Tiffany turned and looked at her daddy. She could not speak. The breathing tube had hurt her throat and it was hard to swallow, let alone talk. A tear spilled out over her long eyelash, but she still smiled.

It was a few days before she was able to talk. Her once vibrant voice was raspy and forced. She asked for water, ate ice chips, and every now and then openly wished for chicken nuggets. Tom never left the hospital. The nurses were kind enough to roll in a cot for him to sleep on and they gave him some scrubs to wear.

Tiffany didn't talk much. Tom read her stories, asked if she wanted to watch television, which she never did, and sang her grandpa's silly songs to the best of his ability. He would mess up the words, Tiffany would laugh briefly and the laugh would trail off to a high-pitched hiss. During one of those songs, she finally asked for something other than water and chicken nuggets.

"Daddy, will you call Grandma and Grandpa and ask them to come see me?"

"Of course I will."

It was something he was putting off for a reason. They knew she was in the hospital. He had called and told them when he brought Tiffany in. However, they didn't know the severity of the situation and it was fear that kept him from making the call. Like Tom, they would be devastated. Moreover, when one made those calls, it was usually a sign of the end, something he could not bear. Burying a child is awful and it was just as awful to bury a grandchild. He could not bring himself to do it, but now, Tiffany had asked and, of course, he would.

It was the second hardest phone call he had ever made. The first, of course, was the call he placed telling them that Sarah had passed away. Her death had been such a surprise that they did not have time to say goodbye.

Tom left the room and went to an empty visitor's lounge to make the call. He dialed his cell and hesitated before hitting the call button then pressed it. It rang twice before Sarah's mother answered.

"Hello?"

"Hi, Marge," Tom said. "It's me."

"Tommy," she said. Marge and Stu were the only ones that called him Tommy. "How is our little girl?"

Tom gripped the phone and held back the shakiness in his voice before answering.

"She's, uh, she's not well."

There was silence on the other end. He could tell she was holding her breath.

"Doctors said that the cancer has spread to her brain and..."

There was an audible gasp on the other end and Tom heard her hand the phone off to Stu.

"Tommy, what's wrong?" Stu asked.

"It's Tiffany. She wants you two to come up and see her."

"Marge is crying, Tommy."

Tom spoke with a quiver in his voice, "She's not doing well. The cancer spread to her brain and, uh, she's... It's not good, Stu. Tiffany asked for you guys." He barely breathed those last words.

"We'll fly out tonight."

They spent the next fifteen minutes talking about everything that Doctor Mehta told Tom. Stu, the silent strong type that he was, kept calm and talked in a steadfast way. After Tom said goodbye, he broke down in the visitor's lounge and wept. He didn't want to see their faces. He didn't want to witness the despair of others. He was trying to cope with his own.

When Tom returned to Tiffany's room, she was sitting up. He could see that she was in pain and he asked if she wanted him to get a nurse.

"I can't feel my legs, Daddy. It's weird."

Doctor Mehta said she would experience

such. The lesions on her spine would most likely block some nerves, rendering certain limbs useless at times. Tom did not tell Tiffany this. He instead rubbed her legs for her and asked if she would like to hear a story.

"How Sam Hart Beat the Devil," Tiffany said.

"I don't have the book with me, honey."

Tiffany's eyes grew bigger and her bottom lip pouted. Tom smiled and said, "I'll do my best."

Tom told the story of Sam Hart and of how he beat the devil in a horse race and won the devil's horse. For the life of him, Tom didn't understand why Tiffany liked the story so much. It was a simple tale and it was short, but then again, she was only in kindergarten, so simple and short was probably exactly the reason why she liked it.

When he finished, Tiffany was caught between sleep and awake. He sat back in his chair and she opened her eyes and turned to him.

"Daddy?"

"Yes, baby."

"Will you help me write a story?"

"What kind of story?"

Tiffany thought long and hard. "I had a dream once..."

"Yes."

"About angels and Mommy was there, too."

Tom felt a lump form in his throat, but he managed a smile. "That sounds like a good dream."

"It was." Her eyes closed and she said, "They were everywhere."

Then she drifted off to sleep.

CHAPTER FOURTEEN

Stu and Marge Kent took the latest flight out of Tampa and arrived in Detroit at ten forty-two in the morning. They had a layover in Atlanta. Tom stood at the bottom of the escalator in the luggage claim area to greet them both. He shook Stu's hand and Stu grabbed Tom on the shoulder and squeezed. The last time they saw each other was Christmas and it ended on such a happy note. Now, on a brink of a bright summer day, the note had soured.

Marge fell apart as she hugged Tom and ruined his shirt with her smeared mascara. She said something, but Tom couldn't understand her. He hugged her back until she calmed down.

Marge insisted on going straight to the hospital to see Tiffany. Tom agreed and Stu approved with a grunt. She asked many questions. Tom answered to the best of his ability, but the one question she kept on asking was "How is she feeling?" Tom was gracious and answered with "She's doing well" and "She's doing as well as expected," but by the third time, he was aggravated and his grace had waned.

"I don't know what you want me to tell you, Marge. She's dying, so she's not feeling well, okay? What more can I say? She's dying."

It went quiet after that and Tom looked in his rearview mirror and saw Stu's look of disappointment. Out of the corner of his eye, he saw the hurt on Marge's face.

Tom let out a heavy sigh. "I'm sorry."

Marge reached over and put her hand on his.

"It's okay. I'm sorry," she said. "I know you're tired."

Tom nodded then looked in his rearview mirror. Stu had moved on and was looking out the window at the passing scenery.

At the hospital, Marge tiptoed into Tiffany's room, hunched her shoulders, and smiled wide for her granddaughter. Tiffany was awake, she reached out to her grandma, and they hugged. Marge kissed her all over her face. Tiffany let out a raspy giggle. Grandpa snapped his fingers and quietly sang a silly song, much to the delight of little Tiffany. Then he did a little jig for her. She wiggled in her bed and when he finished, he gave her a big bear hug.

"How's the little pumpkin?" Stu said.

"This isn't Disneyworld, Grandpa."

Stu raised his eyebrows and shrugged then said, "You got me there, kiddo."

They stayed for about three hours and played Go Fish, although Tiffany's energy level crashed about an hour and a half into the visit. They all sat with her, talked quietly, and played with her thin head of hair and told stories about the latest happenings around the retirement park where they lived.

As they walked down the hall to the elevators, Stu said, "She's a trooper just like her mom," then Marge broke down in tears and he wrapped his arm around her and they walked the rest of the way huddled like that, Marge crying on Stu's shoulder.

In the lobby, Tom gave Stu the car keys and asked that he bring him back a change of clothes. Marge said they would be back in the morning and Tom waved as they walked out the door and passed the bench where Melissa would sit for her lunch and Tom thought about her. He turned away and went back to the elevators.

The elevator doors opened and there was Melissa. She looked up at Tom and smiled then quickly looked away and walked out, barely giving Tom a chance to react.

"Melissa."

She stopped then turned around, "Hi, Tom."

"How are you?"

"I'm good. You?"

"Tiffany's not doing well."

Melissa's head tilted to the side and her eyes softened, giving Tom a look of concern then she said, "I'm sorry to hear that."

"It's spread to her brain and..."

Melissa moved closer to him and said, "Are you all right?"

"No. I'm not."

She hugged him, much to his surprise. He could smell her perfume. Lavender. It was sweet and it felt nice to hold her.

"If there's anything I can do," she said.

"I appreciate it."

Melissa rubbed his arm, smiled, then turned and walked away.

"Melissa?" She stopped and looked at him. "I'm sorry for standing you up."

She nodded then turned and continued walking. Tom watched her round a corner then he stepped onto the elevator.

In Tiffany's room, Tom plopped down in his chair and saw the notebook that he bought for Tiffany's story. He picked it up and opened it. She wrote "Tiffany" at the top. Below the title, she drew a picture of an angel with wings on a cloud. The angel was looking down, not up and its smile was slanted. Tom chuckled then sat back to take a nap.

It started out low, almost a hum, and then it grew louder, a shrill that pierced his eardrums, like a tornado siren on the first Saturday of the month, "Tooooooooooom!"

His eyes snapped open and he gasped. The room was dark and it was cold. Tiffany was asleep, the machines stacked near her bed beeping, chiming, and blinking. Tom sat up and stretched. His mouth was dry and he smacked his lips, trying to work up some moisture but got nothing. He stood and stared down at Tiffany. Her hands were folded and resting on her chest. She breathed in short bursts of four then one long breath. Tom leaned down and kissed her forehead. He felt the coolness of her skin. He pulled the blanket up around her neck and tucked it in.

Tom walked out into the hallway. It was dark. A few scattered lights overhead strained against the darkness. Down at the end, where the nurse's station was, he saw a lone doctor writing on a chart. He looked up and Tom waved. The doctor went back to his work without an acknowledgment. Tom walked down to the kitchenette on the opposite end of the hallway.

The kitchenette was a small wet bar with snacks, coffee, and cold drinks for parents that spent countless hours holding vigil at the bedside of their sick children. Tom entered and rummaged through the refrigerator for a Coke, but settled for an RC Cola instead. He popped the tab and took a swig then quickly spat it out into the sink. The cola was flat, warm, and syrupy, but the can was cold and it popped and fizzed when he opened it. Tom soured his face and shook his head then threw the can in the trash. A cup of water would have to do.

He looked through the cupboards for a clean cup, finding none, then cupped his hand and turned the faucet on to at least get a mouth full of something wet that did not taste like an old damp shoe. The faucet chugged and sputtered. No water came out. He tapped the top and twisted the handle, but got nothing. Tom turned the other handle. Nothing.

"Are you kidding me?"

He stepped out into the hallway. The doctor was still at the nurse's station working on a chart. He hated bothering doctors with silly things like a drink of water, but he had no one else to ask. Tom headed for the nurse's station.

He walked down the hallway. Each room was dark as he passed. He came to Tiffany's room, looked, and saw a nurse. She was wearing one of those old school uniforms with the white hat and white stockings and she was standing at the foot of Tiffany's bed, looking down at her. Tom stood outside the door.

"Is everything okay?"

The nurse ignored his question. She stood there, looking down at Tiffany.

"Nurse, is everything okay?"

The nurse turned and looked at Tom and said nothing. She raised her finger to her lips and shushed him. Tom furrowed his brow and stepped back. Something wasn't right. He looked at the nurse's station where the lone doctor worked. He hadn't gotten any closer. The gap widened. It seemed further away. Tom was confused. He looked back at the nurse standing over Tiffany's bed.

"I'm thirsty," he said.

The nurse looked at him. She smiled then nodded her head in the direction of the lone doctor. Tom smacked his lips. He tried to swallow. His mouth was dry. He slowly turned away and started to walk toward the doctor.

It felt like he was walking for miles and the more he walked, the thirstier he became. His lips cracked and the corners of his mouth began to sting. His nostrils flared as they became dryer and his eyes burned. Tom broke into a jog, his breath hot and labored. The air heated up around him.

He jogged for what seemed like hours and still could not close the gap. His heart was beating faster and harder. His stomach cramped. The tips of his fingers hurt, as if needles stabbed into them. Tom looked at his hands. His fingers were cracked and bleeding. He squeezed them into fists and cried out as blood dripped from their grips. Tom panicked and ran as fast as he could toward the lone doctor. The air was hot.

With each step, more pain would come. He looked down and saw that his shoes were bloody. He could hardly breathe. His face burned and his lips scorched. Tom tried to yell out. All he could do was cough a plume of gray dust into the hot air. He ran faster, reaching out to the lone doctor. The gap grew wider. Tom collapsed onto the ground, sliding on the waxed floor with a skid. He cried out in pain. His back arched and he reached out for someone to help him.

A hand grabbed hold of his and Tom looked up and saw the doctor.

"Help me," Tom said.

"You thirst," said the doctor.

"Please, help."

The doctor held out a cup of water and said, "If you drink, you'll never thirst again."

Tom reached for the cup. His bloody fingers only inches away. "I can't," he said.

"You can," said the doctor. "Drink and thirst no more."

A nurse accidentally bumped into the tray next to him and the corner of it hit Tom in the head. He snapped awake, startled and scared.

"I'm sorry, Mr. Hatcher," she said. "Are you okay?"

Tom rubbed the spot on his head. He examined the tips of his fingers. There was no blood or cracks, but his mouth was like a gravel road. He told the nurse he was okay then got up and went into the bathroom for some water.

A splash of cold water then a quick slurp from the faucet and everything was all right. He looked in the mirror. He looked old. It wasn't a face for television anymore. Tom examined his eyes and the lines around his mouth. He studied the pores on his nose and his thin eyebrows. His mother used to tell him how jealous she was of his long eyelashes, but as he gave them a closer look, he didn't notice anything especially long about them. He did notice the dark circles, though and how his eyelids drooped down and out. Tom looked himself in the eyes, trying to see through the pupils, trying to see just how far he could look inside.

CHAPTER FIFTEEN

Stu and Marge arrived at the hospital in the morning as they had promised. Tom changed into some clean clothes and he went downstairs to eat breakfast in the hospital's cafeteria while they sat with Tiffany.

It was raining outside and Tom sat by a window picking at oatmeal and toast. The toast was overdone and the oatmeal not as good as he had hoped. It didn't really matter. He wasn't hungry. It was just what he was supposed to do. His cell phone rang and he answered.

"Tom Hatcher."

"Tom? It's Dan. How are you?"

"I'm good," he lied.

"Really?"

"Well, I could complain, but who's listening?"

"You'd be surprised."

Tom rolled his eyes.

"I hear you're down at the hospital again."

"Word gets around."

"I was wondering if it would be okay for me to come by today to see Tiffany and maybe pray with you guys."

"I'll be here all day."

"I'll see you soon."

Tom clicked the phone off and stuffed it back into his pocket. The rain came down in sheets outside the window and thunder shook the building.

"That all you got to say?"

Upstairs in Tiffany's room, Doctor Mehta sat on her bed pressing on Tiffany's neck and asking her questions about her favorite books and school. Tom walked in and saw Stu reading the paper and Marge looking worried with her hands clasped together, leaning forward in the chair.

"Will I get better, Doctor Mehta?" Tiffany rasped.

"Well, that's why you're here, so we can get you better." Doctor Mehta saw Tom and smiled. She stood and patted
Tiffany on the head then said, "You just rest and I'll talk to your father about how we can do that. Okay?"

"Okay."

"It was nice meeting you two," Doctor Mehta said to Stu and Marge.

"Thank you, Doctor," Marge said with that serious and honorable tone she used whenever she spoke to anyone with a title before a name.

Doctor Mehta nodded then walked out of the room with Tom.

"We can start radiation, but I don't recommend chemotherapy. She's too weak for chemo. And surgery is not an option at this point."

"What do you mean surgery isn't an option?"

"The growths are near the base of the brain. It's just not a good spot, Tom. There's no way of going in and getting it without," Doctor Mehta paused, searching for the right words then, "without causing serious damage."

"Meaning, she could die."

"That is a possibility."

Tom shook his head. He no longer could be shocked any further. He had used it all up on the initial news. Now it was all business and care.

"So, now what?"

"So, we do radiation, or..."

"Or, we do nothing," Tom said.

"I was going to say, make her as comfortable as possible." "You mean give up?"

Tom didn't expect her to debate the quality of life with him. It was like arguing over the second coming of Christ. To some it was a good thing, but to others it meant the end of everything they knew and that was a terrifying thought. It was either a new beginning or the ultimate end.

"Do the radiation," Tom said.

Doctor Mehta nodded then said, "Okay. We'll do the radiation."

Tom entered Tiffany's room. Marge napped while Stu did a crossword. Tiffany was drawing a picture in her notebook. Tom lay down next to her.

"Whatchya drawing?"

"People."

Tom saw that she was indeed drawing people. They were all looking up at the angel she had drawn earlier. They had round heads and square bodies.

"Who are they?"

"Everyone."

"Is this part of your story?"

"It's the best part."

"Is that right?"

"Yep!" she rasped and took a deep breath, wheezing as she did.

Tom admired Tiffany for a moment. He studied her eyes. They were her mother's eyes. They were always searching and discovering new things. Her nose was unfortunately his and her lips... well her lips were her own. They were full and pout and as pink as a rose petal. Tiffany carefully colored in some of the people.

"You are a very smart and talented girl."

Tiffany smiled and said, "Thanks, Daddy."

Tom had been sleeping for an hour when he felt someone pull on his foot. He opened his eyes and saw Dan Underwood standing over him. He smiled and Tom saw the Bible cradled in his hand.

"Hey, did I wake you?"

Tom carefully sat up. Tiffany was sleeping and Stu and Marge were sawing logs.

"No, I was exercising. I always do with my eyes shut and in bed."

"I thought so."

Tom stood and they shook hands then walked out of the room and down the hallway to the visitor's lounge. Dan said hi to everyone on the way to the lounge. Some called him by name.

"You get around."

"It's not all preaching and praying. I spend twice the amount of time in hospitals."

"That must be fun."

"Oh, it's the best part of the job." He smiled and they entered the visitor's lounge.

Tom looked around the room at the pictures on the wall. They were the usual sort: landscapes, dolphins, hospitals really liked pictures of dolphins for some reason, and lighthouses. Magazines were scattered on a table in the middle of the room. A television was at the other end, bolted to the stand, so no one would steal it. It was off.

"Not much of a theme," Tom said.

"I think the idea was just throw something on the walls."

"Something to look at."

"Yeah," Dan said. "So, how are you? Is there anything I can do for you? Something the church could do?"

"Don't you usually reserve that for your members?"

Dan laughed then said, "You really have no idea what it is I do, do you?"

Tom was embarrassed, but he managed a grin then shook his head and said, "I guess not."

"So, how are you?"

Tom shrugged.

"I know."

He told Dan about the brain tumor and that surgery was out of the question. Dan listened and asked the right questions at the right moments and Tom continued to spill the beans on Tiffany's situation. Never once did Tom talk about himself.

"I'm sorry to hear all that, Tom."

"It wasn't supposed to be like this."

"It never is."

"That's it? That's all you have to say?"

"I have plenty to say, Tom. I'm just not sure you want to hear it."

Tom rubbed his hand across his face. He was tired, both physically and emotionally.

"The biggest and most unanswerable question man has ever had was and is why," Dan said. "But the real question we should all be asking is what."

"Who cares about the what?"

"But the answer to what makes the why obsolete."

Tom shifted in his seat and crossed his arms. He didn't like where Dan was trying to lead him. He also didn't like jigsaw conversations. Dan wasn't coming right out with it. He was making Tom work for it and he wasn't in the mood. What are we suppose to do, just forget about the bad and only dream of the good in life, he thought.

214

Tainted! Tainted by heavenly psychobabble!

Dan was watching Tom carefully. He finally said, "I know all about the why, Tom. More than I care to."

"Is that so?"

Tom was angry. No, he was more aggravated. He considered Dan a friend, maybe not a good friend, but a friend nonetheless. They established that the other day. He didn't know anyone that would let him dump his emotional garbage on him for the price of nothing. However, Dan could get on his nerves. He was relentless. And they came from two different worlds.

Dan was probably born with a Bible in his hand. All he knew was that perspective, the cloud in the sky, everything happens for a reason look on life. He met people with terrible stories, but he lived in the northern suburbs of Oakland County, far enough from any real trouble. Tom knew. He lived there, too. It was pure Americana and the people that lived there loved it. Tom looked at Dan.

"I haven't talked about this in a long time," Dan said. "But nothing speaks volumes of truth like a man's experience. Against it, there are no arguments. Wouldn't you agree?"

Tom nodded and waited. Dan blew out some nervous energy.

"About seven years ago, I sat in a hospital emergency room asking God why. Why me?" He paused, his eyes looking beyond where they sat now. "Why them? I wasn't always a pastor. I used to work for General Motors. Well, I was a contractor for General Motors. I was married and had two kids."

"Boy and a girl?" Tom asked.

"Two boys. One four and one three. Charles and Jake," Dan said. "I can still hear them laughing during one of their tickle fights on the living room floor." His voice cracked and Tom uncrossed his arms and listened. "Charles was so serious and Jake always the goof. Charles wanted to be an archeologist when he grew up, but Jake wanted to be a pirate." Dan smiled and

216

remembered. "They were good boys."

Tom knew that look. He had seen it too many times in the mirror looking right back at him.

"What happened, Dan?"

Dan came back, the memory leaving him as quickly as it came. He sat back, smirked, and shrugged.

"Car accident. My wife had just picked them up from daycare and was heading to the mall to do some Christmas shopping. She'd told me that the boys wanted to buy me something fun, but they wouldn't tell her what. A combination of ice, a poorly placed salt truck on the side of the road, and a car that was in need of a serious brake job and a guy who didn't know you weren't supposed to drive drunk. They were dead on impact."

The room was silent, but for the hiss of the vent overhead. Tom felt Dan's pain. He watched him and knew that he was recalling that day not only in words, but in his heart and soul, too.

"I sat in the emergency room, my wife and two boys were dead, and suddenly I was all alone. I had questions. Man, did I have questions."

"Is this where you tell me that Jesus answered all of your questions? Because, if it is, how about putting in a good word for me with the head honcho?"

Dan grinned. He leaned toward Tom and said, "He didn't answer any of them. Not a single one. My family was dead. The drunk who killed them was perfectly fine. I was angry and God was silent."

Tom leaned toward Dan and said softly, "Then what can you do for me?"

"You're my friend and I wanted to tell you that I eventually found life again. I remarried. She had two boys of her own, they love me and I love them. It took a while, but life repaired itself. You know what I mean?"

Tom's aggravation instantly turned to anger. The audacity of Dan's conclusion was too much. He furrowed his brow then in a low and seething voice said, "You came here to tell me that life will go on?"

Dan sat straight and held up his hands then said, "I didn't mean it that way."

Tom stood and looked down at Dan and said, "My little girl is down the hall dying and you tell me that you found life again? Are you kidding me? You want me to think about finding life again?"

Dan stood and said, "That's not why I'm here!"

"Then why are you here?" Tom shouted.

"That's the question I asked seven years ago. Why am I here? And then a few weeks back, I finally asked God, what do you want me to do? It seems silly. I gave him my life, went to Bible College, and became a pastor. Wasn't I already doing everything for him?"

Tom narrowed his eyes and asked, "Well, did he answer?"

"He did," Dan said, nodding. He folded his hands together.

Tom saw a twinkle in Dan's eye and he knew that he wanted him to ask what it was that God told him. So, he did.

"Nothing," Dan said as he sat back down with a satisfied look on his face. "It's what he did."

Tom waited for it. Dan was letting it hang there for Tom to wonder and he knew it. He laughed and shook his head.

"I sure wish you would cut to the chase, preacher."

Dan smiled then said, "He sent you, Tom. He sent you on an ordinary Sunday morning with a wake-up call. At the time, I didn't realize that when you hit me, that it was God, but soon he revealed it to me. An answer to my question and when he answered my 'what now' question, he also answered the 'why me.'"

Tom rolled his eyes then stood. He looked

at his hand, the one that knocked Dan to the floor before his entire congregation. The same hand wrote love letters to Sarah when he was in college. The same hand placed a ring on Sarah's finger the day he asked her to marry him. The same hand held Tiffany's tiny finger the day she was born. The same hand brushed Sarah's hair off her forehead while she laid in a coffin at Wints Funeral Home. This was the hand that Dan was now telling him God used to answer his prayers. The thought was ridiculous and Tom laughed.

He turned to Dan and said, "So, let me follow your logic. God killed your family so I could punch you in the face at church and you could help me in my darkest hour. Is that about right?"

Dan became serious again and he looked at Tom with the kind of intensity with which one would look at someone who was about to walk out into a minefield and said, "He didn't kill my family. Bad things happen. It's the world we created. But he does use the bad things to bring about good. That's a fact."

"That's a belief. Not a fact. Not the same."

"It is the same. That's why I'm here."

Tom sat back down. He looked at his hand, chuckled, and then was silent.

And that was it. Dan didn't push the subject any further. Whatever it was, call it the Holy Spirit or a gut reaction, Dan took it as far as it would go. They went to Tiffany's room where Marge was reading her a story and Stu was still sawing logs. Marge stopped when she saw Tom and Dan enter and she stood and folded her hands and bowed her head slightly then said, "Oh, hi, Pastor."

Dan shook her hand and told her how nice it was to see her again.

Tom asked, "You met?"

"This morning. When I stopped by your house."

"I didn't know you were friends with a minister, Tom," Marge said.

"Well..."

"It's not that big of a deal, Mrs. Kent," Dan said. "I'm just a shmoe whose job just happens to be teaching the Bible."

"Oh, I don't know about that. Some people take that stuff very seriously," Marge said.

"Yes, I suppose they do."

Tom knew as well as Marge did that she couldn't care less about some minister. This holy mother act was getting on his nerves. Marge believed in God just as she believed in Santa. Put a few drinks in her and she would tell you exactly how she felt about Jesus and the church, thought Tom. He decided to change the subject before her groveling idea of respect got out of hand and Tom lost his patience.

"Why don't you and Dad go get some lunch?"

Marge nodded and looked over at Stu with his head back and mouth open, snoring like some wino on a park bench. She sheepishly looked at Dan and smiled then said, "It's been a long night." Then she walked over to Stu, nudged him, and said, "Stu? Dear, let's go for some lunch."

Stu grumbled and continued to snooze. Marge nudged him again and said lightly, "Stu, dear. Honey, wake up." She looked at Dan and blushed. She then slapped Stu on the shoulder and barked, "Stuart!"

Stu snapped out of his slumber and brushed her away then said, "Good god, woman, give me a chance."

"Let's get some lunch, Stu," Marge said.

He still had one foot in dreamland and Marge slapped him on his shoulder and said, "Stu!"

He was fully awake now and he shot a look up at Marge and said, "I swear!"

Marge offered that sheepish smile to Dan again. Dan smiled and nodded, reassuring her that it was quite all right. Marge grabbed her purse then Stu's arm and yanked him out of the chair and they walked out of the room. When it was safe, Dan let out a hearty laugh and sat down.

"I'm sorry about that. My mother-in-law tends to, I don't know, turn into a geisha around certain people."

"It's all right. She means well."

Tom shrugged and Dan shook his head and said, "They really are good people, though."

"They are."

Tiffany cleared her throat and they both looked at her and she said in her raspy voice, "Um, aren't you here to see me?"

Tom laughed and Dan walked over to her bedside and sat on the edge, "Why, yes I am and I'm sorry you felt ignored."

Tiffany beamed and patted Dan on the hand then said, "Oh, that's okay. I forgive you."

She showed Dan her notebook. She told him about the story of Sam Hart and about how she was going to write a story about Tiffany Hatcher. Dan gave his approval, much to her satisfaction, and Tom watched and admired his daughter as she continued to go on and on about the book.

"Pastor Dan? Why did they tell us to leave the church?"

Dan's gaze went from Tiffany to the floor then back to Tiffany; his face revealed his shame and he said, "That shouldn't have happened. Big Mac is sorry he did that."

"Big Mac?" laughed Tiffany.

Dan chuckled then said, "I know. It's a silly name, but he's a really nice guy."

Tiffany fiddled with her fingers and started to color her book again then she said, "What's heaven like?"

"Tiffany," Tom said

"What, Daddy?"

Tom didn't respond. He couldn't. He sat there, thinking this was it. This was the downward spiral. All that there was to this little life, as if the hereafter was all that remained, was all there was to discuss. It made me sick to his stomach.

"Well, Tiffany," Dan said. "It's a lot like here only there isn't any sickness and everybody is happy."

Tiffany thought about it for a moment. She said, "I don't wanna be sick no more."

Tom held his breath. He waited for it to pass, his heart sinking, his mind melting. He realized that Tiffany was preparing herself and he couldn't bear it, because he wasn't prepared. He would never be prepared.

Dan looked at Tom then took Tiffany's hand and held it then said, "Would it be all right if I pray with you?"

She nodded and Dan placed his hand on her head and said, "Dear God, touch this life and make her whole. I ask for healing and

peace in the name of Jesus, and bless this
family. I thank you for all that you have
done, all that are doing, and all that you will
do. Amen."

Tiffany looked up at Dan and said,
"Amen." Then she smiled.

CHAPTER SIXTEEN

Tiffany died on a Sunday. Her funeral was on a Tuesday. As per her wishes, they held the service at Dan Underwood's church. They had become good friends. Tom's coworkers from the station were there, as well as most everyone from the church. Tom was inconsolable.

The radiation treatments did little to help her. She grew worse with each passing day. Within a month, she was home with hospice care and Tom had the hospital bed that he ordered set up in the sun room so that she could see the ducks in Old Mill Pond. She talked often about the ducks and she worried that there was no one that would feed them when she was gone. Tom promised that he would make sure that they were well taken care of and not to worry.

Dan visited every day. He spent most of his time with Tiffany. Now and then, Tom would sit with them both, as they talked about Dan's church, heaven, and even the ducks. Most of the time, Tom left them alone. It was Tiffany's time to visit with her friend. He felt useless on matters of the spirit anyway and it broke his heart not to be able to satisfy her questions.

On that terrible Sunday, the morning sun reflected off Old Mill Pond. The ducks were close to the house and Tiffany could hear them quacking. Sarah's parents were there with her, too. Tom sat on the edge of the bed while Marge and Stu stood. They were anticipating the moment.

"Why are they quacking, Daddy?" Tiffany's voice was a little more than a whisper.

Tom looked out the window and saw four ducklings waddling toward the house where the older mallards waited.

"They're calling their babies, Tiff."

"Are they sad?"

Tom watched the ducklings join the older mallards and the mother duck nestled her bill in the wings of her ducklings, making them squeak and quack.

"No, Honey, they're very happy."

She was satisfied and soon thereafter, little Tiffany, a mere six and a half years old, almost seven, slipped from this world to the next with her father and grandparents by her side and her last words were, "I'm happy."

The next day, on a sweltering Michigan summer afternoon, Tom walked into the studio at work and told Gene that he quit and thanked everyone for their kind letters and cards. When Gene asked him what he would do, he said that he didn't know. The receptionist, whom he barely knew, cried and hugged him as he walked out with a small box of his belongings under his arm.

Wints Funeral Home remembered him by

name and told him how sorry they were for his loss then offered their best package for his daughter. Tom said he would cremate and bury the urn with her mother. They smiled, nodded, and offered their counseling services, of which Tom politely turned down again.

The night before the funeral, Marge had to be sedated while Stu sat quietly by the fireplace, staring into its dark and empty space. Tom was determined to perform the eulogy, a task that would not come easy. He was shocked and too distraught to eulogize Sarah at her funeral and had regretted it since. This time, he would do what was right and properly honor his daughter, even if it took him all night.

Tom sat at his desk in the tiny office just outside of his bedroom staring at a blank legal pad. He had only written one word: Tiffany. Every time he put pen to paper, he cried and lost any thought he was having. Tom sat there writing nothing for over an hour then finally got up and went to her room to look around. He needed something to help him put into words that which he was feeling.

He sat on her bed and smelled her pillow and held one of her many stuffed animals. He looked at the posters and drawings on the wall. He opened and closed her drawers and looked through her closet. Now that she was gone, he wanted to see if missed any part of her life. He wanted to see if he truly appreciated her presence in his life. It was a painful exercise and eventually, he cried himself to sleep in her bed.

When he awoke in the early morning hours, he panicked. Tom had not written a thing and it was now too late. Whatever he wrote now would be rushed and meaningless. The guilt was heavy.

He came down the stairs, showered and shaved. Tom wore his dual-purpose black suit Sarah bought him. "This will cover you for weddings and funerals," she said when he first tried it on. So far, not a single wedding, but two funerals, he thought.

Stu was dressed and sitting at the fireplace. He looked to be in deep thought, so Tom didn't say anything to him. Marge boiled water for her morning tea in the kitchen.

"Morning, Mom."

"That it is, Tom," she said. Marge was a pendulum of emotions. At no time did she ever rest between joy and depression. For obvious reasons, she was on the downswing of depression.

Tom kissed her on the head and she held his cheek, keeping him close for a few seconds more of comfort.

"I'm making tea. Would you like some?"

"I'll take a cup."

He looked out the window facing the backyard and Old Mill Pond. Splashes of sunlight broke through the oak trees in the backyard and the pond shimmered as the family of ducks waddled from the water. Marge poured him a teacup of hot water and asked him if he preferred Earl Grey or English Tea Time.

"Earl Grey," he said and she placed the teabag into the cup and handed it to him. Tom went to the sun room where Tiffany's hospital bed still sat.

The room was bright with morning sun and the flowers that his coworkers sent made it smell like a garden, or a funeral home, depending on your state of mind. No roses, that's all Tom asked. He hated roses. They reminded him of death and he had enough reminders to last him a lifetime.

He sat on Tiffany's bed, sipping his tea, and watching the ducks waddling near the edge of Old Mill Pond. It wasn't long ago that Tiffany chased and fed them, giggling and squealing, scaring the feathers off those ducks. Sarah and Tom sat in this very room and drank Long Island Ice Teas and dreamed of growing old and having Tiffany and her family visit for holidays and birthday parties. Now it was a room for Earl Grey and longing.

Tom sipped his tea and he saw Tiffany's notebook peeking out from under the pillow. He pulled it out and turned the pages. His eyes welled up and the tears rolled down his face as he turned each page. The book was full. It had pictures and thoughts written with help from her friend Dan Underwood. He recognized the handwriting. They were her perspectives and reflections of those she loved most and he realized that he had her eulogy. He had everything that he ever needed for his lovely daughter's eulogy. He couldn't think of a better way to memorialize Tiffany than with her own words.

For the funeral service, a young woman, her name was Lisa, sang a song that Tom had never heard before. Her voice was clear, powerful, and subtle when it needed to be. Big Mac accompanied her on the acoustic guitar. His meaty fingers lightly moved up and down the frets.

Tom sat in the front row, gripping Tiffany's notebook. Stu and Marge sat beside him. No matter how hard he tried, he couldn't hold back the tears. Marge told him it was all right and she hooked her arm around his. As Lisa milked the last note and Big Mac picked the final chords, there wasn't a dry eye in the place. A hand gripped Tom's shoulder from behind then patted him on the back. He looked back to see Gene with tears in his eyes. Tom nodded and mouthed "thanks."

Dan took the stage and paused briefly before speaking. He looked at the picture of Tiffany framed on a table next to him. It was her school picture. It was her only school picture. Her face graced with a wide and toothy grin. Her eyes were bright as only a child's could be. He cleared his throat and looked out at all of the mournful faces staring back up at him.

"Death cancels all things but memories."

Dan watched the people nod and wipe away tears. He looked down at Tom in the front row. Tom's eyes were down and he gripped the notebook closely to his chest. Stu held Marge tightly to his side, his arm wrapped around her shoulders, and her eyes smeared with mascara as she dabbed at them with a handkerchief. Dan took a deep breath and sighed heavily.

"Thank God for those memories. Even

though we know and take heart that Tiffany Hatcher, a girl that has gone from this world to the next too soon, is more alive than we could ever imagine. Those memories help keep her alive here in our hearts and in our minds.

"I was lucky enough to meet Tiffany about a month ago. In that short period, she was the one that spoke into my life and I'm blessed to have known her. But it is her father, Tom Hatcher, that will keep her memory alive. At this time, he's going to share with you the story of his baby girl. Tom?"

Tom stood and walked up the polished wooden stairs leading up to the stage. He stopped at the table bearing Tiffany's picture and he picked up the photograph and kissed it then placed it gently back on the table. The photo was surrounded by the flowers that were in the sun room of the house and Tom breathed deeply, closed his eyes, and imagined that he was in the room with Tiffany again as she wrote the words in her notebook and drew the pictures around them.

The sun shone brightly and the flowers added splashes of color around the room. Tiffany lay in her bed, a yellow blanket pulled up to her knees, her stuffed animals snuggled in her arms. She was adding to her final page and as she made the last stroke of the crayon, she held the notebook up to admire her work and smiled.

"There, Daddy! It's all done."

Tom turned away from the window. He was watching the ducks waddle along the bank of Old Mill Pond. He turned to look at Tiffany, aglow in the sunlight, smiling and holding up her notebook for him to see the cover she had made for it. He stepped over to her side and took the notebook.

The cover was the finished picture of the Angel on the cloud that looked down at all of the people. A rainbow arced above her. Trees reached out from the edge of the page. A pond, probably Old Mill Pond, shimmered in blue in the background, and Tom could see yellow ducks on the bank. They were looking up, too. A dozen or so people were standing below the angel and looking up.

Some were waving, some were smiling, and some had sad faces. Above the angel was a star with a cloud ring around it and beside the star was a woman in yellow and a hallo above her head. Across the top of the page was the title: Tiffany.

"Do you want me to read it to you, Daddy?"

"I hope that you would," Tom said as he handed the notebook back to Tiffany.

She beamed a grin and opened the notebook with the fervor of a Christmas morning. Tom sat on the edge of the bed and she began.

"This is a story about me. My name is Tiffany Hatcher, I am six and a half years old, and I have cancer. My mommy had cancer and she died and I'm going to go see her in heaven. But, this isn't a sad story. Well, it's kind of sad, because Daddy will be sad.

"This is a happy story. These are happy thoughts and happy wishes."

Tiffany turned the book to show Tom the pictures she had drawn around the words that she had dictated. There were purple horses, red and blue hot air balloons, funky music notes, rainbows, and yellow ducks.

"Those are the things I like, Daddy."

"It's very good, honey. Keep reading."

Tiffany turned the page and read, "We live in Michigan and there's a pond in our backyard and we have ducks. It's a duck family. I like to chase them and they like to chase me. I think we're best friends.

"We live in a big house and my daddy is on TV. My mommy was a mommy and she was the best mommy, too. We did everything together and we always laughed."

She turned the book to show the pictures of Tom and Sarah holding their bellies and the word's "Ha! Ha!" in word bubbles. A picture of Tiffany with her hands on her hips and a scowl on her face with water dripping off her was at the bottom of the page. The

yellow ducks were splashing water on her
from the pond and had "Quack! Quack!" in
word bubbles above them.

Tom smiled approvingly and Tiffany
turned the page.

"When Mommy got sick, everybody
stopped laughing. We were all sad. Daddy
cried in his sleep."

She showed Tom the picture of him in bed
with tears coming out and she was on her
knees praying by a window. Tiffany turned
the page.

"I asked God to make us happy again and
to help Daddy. We started playing again."

She turned the book and this time it was a
picture of Tom holding his belly and the
words "Ha! Ha!" in a word bubble above
him and Tiffany was down at the bottom of
the page laughing and splashing water on
the yellow ducks.

"You see what I did?"

"I see it, honey."

She turned the page and read, "Then I got sick." Tiffany showed the picture of her with a frown on her face and a bandage on her forehead. She looked up at Tom and said, "Don't worry, Daddy. It gets better."

"Okay, baby girl."

She continued reading. "Daddy was very sad and he was very mad. He yelled at God a lot and I told God he was sorry a lot." She looked at Tom before continuing. He nodded and she turned the page.

"One day I had a dream about angels and Mommy." Tiffany turned the page without looking to her dad for approval.

"They told me that Daddy would be all right and Mommy said that I was a very good girl and we would have lots of fun and not to be afraid. When I woke up, I wasn't afraid, but I was sad because Daddy was sad." She turned the page.

Tom took a deep breath. Tears pooled in

his eyes and his lip quivered. A lump formed in his throat. She waited for it to pass then she said to Tom, "It'll be all right, Daddy." He nodded and she continued to read.

"One day, Pastor Dan came to see me and we talked about heaven and Jesus and angels. Pastor Dan said that angels are our helpers and that they are all around. I told him I saw an angel once." Tiffany turned the page.

"I wish that everybody is good and nice to everyone. I wish that my ducks will be okay and not miss me as much as I will miss them. I wish Daddy would be happy. Maybe someday he will find a girl to marry again and I will have brothers and sisters. And I wish Daddy will never forget about Mommy and me. We'll be in heaven waiting for him."

Tiffany looked up at her daddy. Tears rolled down his cheeks. She smiled at him then said, "The end." Tiffany closed the notebook. "Did you like it?"

In a low whisper marred with tears and a

suppressed sob, Tom said, "I liked it very much."

Tom looked up at the mourners seated in the church. He saw people dab their eyes, wipe their noses, and put their arms around their loved ones. Tom managed a smile through the tears he was crying, as well. He placed his hands upon the notebook.

"My daughter was an angel. She has always been one. Everyday spent with her was a tiny glimpse into heaven. She made me smile when I was sad and she was so smart and would often challenge my stubborn heart. I loved her very much and I'm going to miss her more than I could ever explain to her or anyone."

Tom picked up the notebook, walked off the stage to his seat and sat down. He didn't make eye contact with anyone. This was a private moment in a crowded room. This was a moment between him and Tiffany. Everyone else was a spectator. He held the notebook close to his chest as Dan took the stage to complete the service.

Graveside, Stu recited Tiffany's favorite silly song without shedding a single tear and without any sign of wavering in his voice. He was purposeful and stoic. Upon the last word of the silly song lyric, Stu simply walked away. He walked all the way back to Tom's house, just two miles from Tiffany's final resting place.

The church held a luncheon for those that wanted to stick around and offer their condolences to the family. Tom made his appearance only after he dropped Marge off at his home and gave her two pills that Doctor Mehta gave him to help him sleep at night. As he closed the door to the guest room to give Marge privacy, he saw Stu lying on Tiffany's bed, hugging a stuffed horse. His eyes were wide open and he staring at the ceiling. Tom closed the door to her room without checking on him and headed back to the church.

Big Mac was the first one to see Tom walk in and he immediately went up to him and said how sorry he was for his loss. Tom thanked him and said that he played the guitar very well. Big Mac thanked him then

Tom made his way around the room, shaking hands and saying thank you. He had just shook the hand of the man with the mutton chops when he felt a tap on his shoulder. He turned to see Doctor Mehta.

Doctor Mehta hugged him and said, "She was a wonderful little girl. I wish we could've done more."

"You did everything you could. Thank you."

"A few of the other doctors and some of the nurses came up to pay their respects. Everyone really loved her."

"I know. Please, let everyone know how much I appreciate everything they did for my girl, okay? You know, in case I don't get a chance to."

"Of course, Tom," Doctor Mehta said. She touched his shoulder and offered a kind smile.

Tom watched her walk to the other side of the room and that was when he saw Melissa.

She was in the middle of an engrossing conversation, judging by the intense look on her face. Suddenly, her face lit up, she smiled brightly, and Tom smiled, too. He had forgotten how he really enjoyed her company and he heard her laugh through the crowded room.

Dan walked up to Tom and gripped him by the elbow. Tom jumped a little then turned around with a surprised look on his face.

"Sorry about that," Dan said. "Didn't mean to get you."

"Caught me daydreaming."

"Can we talk?"

Tom looked around the room at all the faces he had yet to greet and thank.

"As long as there's chicken and green bean casserole they'll be here," Dan said. "Come on."

Tom smiled. Dan had a way with words

and he knew how to ease a mind. He followed Dan upstairs to his office.

"I have something for you. Have a seat."

Tom sat down. Dan sat at his desk and opened a drawer. He pulled out a Bible and set it on the desk.

"This is a Bible, Tom."

"I can see that."

"But, it's no ordinary Bible. This is a very special book. Probably more special than any Bible you'll ever hold in your hand."

Tom grinned and crossed his legs then said, "Okay, Dan."

"I'm serious." He opened the Bible and began to read. "Dear Daddy..."

Tom's face slacked. Tears welled up in his eyes and he uncrossed his legs and sat straight in the chair.

Dan continued. "Merry Christmas, happy

birthday, and all that good stuff. This is for you, because you're the best. Love, Tiffany. P.S., goodlovdo: it means, doing love good. I love you."

Dan looked up at Tom and said, "She had me write that. There's more." Dan continued to read. "Dear Tom, you gave your daughter a good life and now it's time to do the same for yourself. This isn't just any ordinary book. It's a toolbox with instructions on how to get the best out of life. You were an amazing father and you are a good man.

"I know that it's been a tough couple of years, but the worst is behind you, while the best is ahead of Tiffany. She loved you very much, but her love is nothing compared to the love God has for you. So, use this book wisely, my friend. Yours truly, Dan Underwood."

Dan closed the Bible and looked up at Tom, his face wet with the tears that would not stop.

"When I asked her if there was anything that she wanted me to do for you, she said to give you a Bible. She was a very special girl, Tom."

Dan slid the book toward Tom and picked it up, opened it, and ran his fingers across the inscription and reread it to himself.

"I asked her what she wanted more than anything and Tiffany said that she wanted her daddy to be happy. Are you happy, Tom?"

Tom shook as he silently cried. Tears dropped on the pages of the Bible and he said, "I'm lost."

"We all are. When my wife and boys died, I realized for the first time how utterly alone I was and how lost. In that moment, I knew I wouldn't make it without help and God came running toward me."

Dan stood and walked around to his bookshelf and lifted the statuette of the soul breaking free from its bronzed skin. He held it in his hand then said, "He ran to me, Tom. He lifted me up and told me everything was all right and that I could be free. It wasn't easy. It wasn't even a little bit hard. It was a journey through deep valleys and dark days."

Dan gripped the statuette. He sat down next to Tom then held it out for Tom to take and said, "A very good friend gave this to me when I gave my life over to God, as a symbol of that freedom. I want you to have it now."

Tom looked through the tears at the statuette called "Born Again." He wanted to grab hold of it, but something inside of him was screaming not to. His heart raced and he could feel his stomach twist in knots.

Then Dan said, "Everything within you is telling you no right now. I know. But God is running toward you and all you have to do is say yes." He paused for a moment, watching Tom. "Take it, Tom."

Tom stared at the statuette then back to the inscriptions written in the Bible. He finally whispered, "What do I do?"

"Ask Jesus into your heart and take that

first step forward."

"I'm afraid."

"Don't be afraid. Choose life, Tom."

Tom gripped the Bible, the tears flowing, his heart pounding. He took hold of the statuette then whispered, "To die is to live."

Tears fell from Dan's eyes and he smiled and said, "God, help us all and help my brother. There is a season for everything. I know this. Help Tom in this season of his life. Comfort him and give him hope. Forgive him of his sins and lift him up."

He released the statuette and Tom broke down, sliding off the chair onto his knees. Dan knelt beside him and embraced Tom and they cried together. Like a newborn baby, they cried until they could cry no more.

An hour had passed when Tom and Dan finally emerged from his office. Tom held the Bible and statuette in his arm and they stood at the top of the stairs going down to the main floor where the luncheon was still going on.

"Thanks, Dan. For everything."

"No. Thank you, Tom. Today, three prayers were answered: mine, Tiffany's, and now yours."

Tom's eyes dropped to the floor then back up at Dan and he smiled and said, "I know."

Dan hugged Tom then watched him walk down the stairs and he thanked God for answered prayers then went back to his office.

CHAPTER SEVENTEEN

Tom walked into the room where there was still some stragglers hanging around talking and even laughing. He looked around, but didn't see the person he was looking for. She had left and he regretted that he didn't get a chance at least to say hi.

He made sure to speak with those he missed before he went upstairs with Dan. Tom thanked them for coming, told stories about Tiffany, and managed even to eat some chicken and green bean casserole. Finally, he decided it was time to go home.

There was a red Ford Focus in the driveway and he parked behind it. He'd never seen it before and stopped on his way to the front door to peek inside of the car. It was clean, nothing to give him a hint of who it was. Tom climbed the steps to the front door and entered the house.

Immediately, he smelled lavender when he entered. He heard talking in the kitchen then that familiar laugh. Tom placed the statuette and Bible on a table by the stairs and headed to the kitchen.

At the table sat Stu, Marge, and Melissa. They were drinking coffee. Marge was smiling. She had her hand on top of Melissa's hand. Stu saw Tom first.

"Well, there he is now."

Melissa and Marge turned to see Tom. Melissa's eyes lit up. She smiled. Tom felt his heart do that funny little dance it did when they first met and he said profoundly, "Hi."

"Hi."

Marge stood and nudged Stu. He followed suit, stood, and walked out of the room. Marge hugged Tom and whispered in his ear, "She's a nice girl, Tom." She then kissed him on the cheek and followed Stu out on to the front porch where they sat and watched the traffic drive by and neighbors walk their dogs.

Tom looked at Melissa. She stirred her coffee and he sat down next to her and said, "I saw you at the luncheon."

"I know. I saw you, too, but you left with the pastor before I could get over to you." She finished stirring her coffee then looked into his eyes. "He seems nice."

Tom nodded then said, "He might be my best friend."

She chuckled. "Might be?"

Tom chuckled, too, then said, "It's been a crazy couple of years. I haven't had that much time to make friends."

Melissa nodded thoughtfully and sipped her coffee. Tom stood up and went over to the coffee pot then said, "Let me warm that up for you."

She held the cup out and he poured some hot coffee into it then poured himself a cup and sat back down. They looked at their mugs in silence. Finally, Melissa said, "I don't want anything, Tom. That's not why I am here."

"Yes, it is."

"No, it's not."

"Yes, it is."

She got a perturbed look on her face and she said, "No. It's not."

Tom sipped his coffee and smiled. He could tell that she was aggravated and it made him happy for some reason. He had that affect on women. It was part of his charm. He set his cup down, as did she, and he took her by the hand.

"Melissa, I don't want anything, either. Except, that is, to be your friend and I'm sorry for not being a very good one."

She smiled then looked down into her cup

of coffee and said, "I want to be friends, too."

They sat there, holding hands, and Tom knew he was taking a second step forward.

CHAPTER EIGHTEEN

A year had passed since Tiffany died. The gray seasons of Michigan had come and gone, leaving behind moments of hope in the midst of hurt and wonder. Tom was in Rudy's Market getting a six-pack of Faygo Colas, the kind that needed a bottle opener. He paid the kid behind the counter for the drinks then stepped out onto the sun soaked sidewalk. It was a beautiful summer day and downtown Clarkston was full of people heading to the park just behind the market for a concert. It was Jazz Band Saturday, a favorite of Tom's. He made his way around the corner and walked to the park.

A trio was banging out some Dixie Jazz as Tom wound his way through families and couples on blankets picnicking and watching the show. A clown was entertaining kids not far from the stage. He continued through the crowd to a more secluded spot near the creek that ran through the park and where a large oak tree shaded Melissa waiting for him on a blanket.

She read a book and ate grapes from a picnic basket next to her. She saw Tom, smiled then waved. Tom held up the six-pack of Faygo and she pretended to applaud.

He sat down next to her and said, "The place was packed."

"Did you get a bottle opener?"

Tom fished in his pocket and produced one then said, "We have cream soda, cherry, grape, and plain old cola for those that are plain and old."

Melissa laughed and said, "Cherry, please."

"Coming right up."

Tom popped the top to a bottle of cherry

cola and handed it to Melissa. He then popped the topped to a plain old cola and saw Melissa shake her head and roll her eyes.

"Like I said plain and old."

The trio broke into another song and Tom held up his bottle and said, "To Jazz."

"If you say so."

They clinked bottles and drank. Melissa went back to reading her book as Tom watched her. The sun broke through the oak leaves overhead and highlighted the red in her hair. He liked how she moved her lips as she read and he watched her eyes move from word to word, line by line. She sensed him watching her and a smile formed on her lips.

"Why are you staring at me?"

"Just watching you read."

"Well, watch the band. You'll make them jealous if you don't."

Tom watched her continue reading then moved his gaze to the band. They were playing a light dance tune and an older couple danced near the stage.

"Do you wanna dance?"

Melissa looked up from her book and said, "Do you?"

"Nah."

She went back to her book and Tom decided that this was a good time and he fished in his pocket for the box. He felt the velvet and rubbed his thumb across the top and to the hinge of the box. His heart jumped and instantly his mouth went dry. Tom took a drink of his Faygo cola then sat up and got on one knee.

Melissa, without looking up, said, "You're not going to go dance by yourself, are you? Because, I'm not sure I could handle it."

Tom cleared his throat then said, "Melissa?"

She looked up from her book and saw him on his knee with a black velvet ring box held out in his hand.

"What are you doing?"

"I can't think of anything more that I would want in this life than to have you as my wife."

Melissa let the book slip from her hand and she sat up, her mouth slacked and tears welled up in her eyes. Her heart pounded and her head started to spin. Tom opened the ring box, revealing a one-caret teardrop cut diamond set in platinum.

"Oh, Tom."

"I love you, Melissa. Will you marry me?"

Melissa held out her shaking hand and cried. "Yes, Tom. Yes, I will marry you. With all my heart, I will marry you."

Tom grinned and removed the ring from the box then slid it upon her trembling finger and he said, "This makes me happy."

About the Author

Gary W. Allison resides in Michigan with his wife and is the proud father of two children, now grown and trying to figure out life. He is the author of The Final Round. You can follow him on Twitter to learn of new projects, old projects, and quips about nothingness and tomfoolery.

@gwallison

Made in the USA
Columbia, SC
10 March 2023

13497786R00146